RIVER OF DREAMS

RIVER OF DREAMS

JAN NASH

Roaring Brook Press
New York

Text copyright © 2020 by Jan Nash

Published by Roaring Brook Press

Roaring Brook Press is a division of Holtzbrinck Publishing Holdings
Limited Partnership

120 Broadway, New York, NY 10271

fiercereads.com

Library of Congress Control Number: 2019948806

ISBN: 978-1-250-24884-8

Our books may be purchased in bulk for promotional, educational, or
business use. Please contact your local bookseller or the Macmillan
Corporate and Premium Sales Department at (800) 221-7945 ext. 5442 or by
email at MacmillanSpecialMarkets@macmillan.com.

First edition, 2020

Book design by Aurora Parlagreco

Printed in the United States of America

10 9 8 7 6 5 4 3 2 1

For Liz, who made my dreams possible,
and Abe and Hazel, who made them real

RIVER OF DREAMS

ONE

There was ice and snow everywhere.

So why did Finn feel so hot?

She peeled off her sweatshirt. It was her favorite, soft and frayed at the edges, but as hot as she was, carrying it seemed stupid. She dropped it to the ice and looked around.

How did she get here? And, more important, how was she supposed to get home? A bead of sweat rolled off her lip and into her mouth. Salty. It made her think of pretzels. She was hungry. Why hadn't she packed a snack?

And why did her ankles feel wet?

She looked down and saw that her right foot was in a slushy hole. She pulled it out, but when she set it down again, the ice below her foot melted, and kept melting.

Before she could do anything, the water rose to her ankles, then her shins, finally splashing against her chest. She barely had time to take a breath before she slipped into the ocean below, the ice now a coffinlike ceiling above her.

She was drowning. Dying, without ever doing anything. No college, no pyramids, no Cantonese. She didn't really even know how to drive yet.

Finn's lungs burned with the effort of not breathing. She had to get to the surface. There must be some way to get to the surface.

She looked up and saw—

A boy, floating in a tangle of kelp, a glowing green cord around his neck. She kicked toward him as he slowly spun around, and she saw his face . . . Noah!

Eyes closed. Unconscious. His skin pale and translucent. Drowning, too. Maybe already dead.

She reached out a hand and—

His eyes snapped open.

"Finn! Help me," he pleaded. "Please."

"Noa—"

Water rushed into her mouth, her throat, filling her lungs. Finn thought of her father. He never said goodbye. And now she was leaving without—

Finn sat up, gasping.

She was in her room. On the table next to her, an alarm beeped insistently.

Fahrenheit 451 was on the bed, a pencil marking the spot where she'd given up on it last night. Her jeans were draped on the chair by her desk. The lead singer of Lords of the Playground was pointing from the poster on the door. And the flyer from the Trans-Australia train trip she dreamed of taking was still propped by her computer. Everything was the same as it had been when she'd fallen asleep.

It was just a dream. She didn't have to be afraid of ice, drowning, failing Noah. She could just be afraid of what she was usually afraid of ...

Everything else.

Finn walked barefoot down the hall. There were no lights on in the house. Nana must not be up yet.

She got to the small room off the kitchen and pushed open the door. Her younger brother, Noah, lay on the bed, a blanket pulled up to just below his chin. Eddie—their brown-and-black shepherd-Lab mix—looked up at her from the foot of the bed, where he'd been sleeping. Keeping watch. Not that Noah was going anywhere.

People used to say they looked alike, but Finn never saw it. Where Noah's hair was blacker than a moonless night, hers couldn't decide if it wanted to be dark brown or auburn. They were both thin, but Noah made his slightness seem powerful. And, while Finn had the Driscoll green eyes, Noah's were piercingly blue. If he would just wake up and get out of bed, every girl in his freshman class would fall in love with him.

Noah had gone into a coma nine months ago, right after his fourteenth birthday. There was no warning—no bad reaction to food or drugs, no blow to the head, no loss of oxygen. One morning he just didn't wake up.

Finn and her mother, Julia, had ridden to the hospital in

the ambulance. The EMT kept asking them questions: "Did he hit his head . . . Was he anaphylactic . . . a drug user?" No, no, and no. Nothing. He just didn't wake up. Her mother cried and tried to hold his hand, but the EMT kept taking it back to insert a needle or check his blood pressure. The sounds—the ripping of sterile packages and beeping equipment—it was all so loud. Finn started humming, trying to drown it out.

At the hospital, they took him away. Scans, blood tests, more scans. More questions about what he might have done, what might have caused it? Specialists came and ordered more tests, sometimes the same test, but none of it mattered.

It all came back "normal." Noah was healthy, they said . . . except for being unconscious.

Nana came to help, and the three of them—Finn, her mother, and Nana—took turns staying at the hospital. When Finn was home, she'd go to her room, put on headphones, and play music as loudly as she could until the pounding in her ears drowned out the silence.

After a month with no change, they brought him home. They put him in the room off the kitchen because it fit the hospital bed better. Mom decorated with stuff from his bedroom: drawings and vintage video game posters, a shelf full of graphic novels. It was like a replica of Noah's real bedroom, just like how the unresponsive boy on the bed seemed like a replica of her real brother. Finn hated it.

The floor was cold on her feet as she crossed to her brother's bed. "Good morning, shrimp." She leaned down and gave him a kiss on the cheek. "You were in my dream last night. I was hot and melted through ice, and you were floating in the ocean."

She brushed the hair from his eyes and waited to see if he'd respond . . . a twitch, a smile, a sigh. There was nothing.

A nurse came to check on him every day. The physical therapist came three times a week. Her mom, who was an expert in underwater construction, had taken a job with a Norwegian oil company to get better benefits, so much of the work of caring for Noah fell to Finn and her grandmother. They fed, bathed, and turned him so he wouldn't get sores. Finn did her homework in his room, working through math problems (she could have used his help) or discussing the novels from English class (if he were conscious, he would have left the room). She even told him things she would never say if he were awake. Like about Marcus Hahn, who sat next to her in biology.

She watched him quietly breathing in and out. Finn didn't let herself think about Noah before the coma. But seeing him in her dream . . .

Tears welled up in her eyes. She wiped them away with her sleeve. Even though she knew he couldn't see her, at the hospital she'd always left his room and cried someplace else. After a few weeks, she willed herself to stop crying and hadn't since. *Must be the dream*, she thought. She stood up. "I'll get you some breakfast."

In the kitchen, she grabbed an IV bag of liquid food to hook up to Noah's gastric tube.

"Good morning, Fionnuala."

Her grandmother, Margaret, was the only person in the world who dared to call her by her real name. "Good morning, Nana."

"How is Noah this morning?"

"He wants bacon for breakfast."

Nana smiled.

"And, I think I forgot to tell you, I'll be late getting home from school. My group's meeting to work on our science project."

"It's Monday."

Monday was the day they called her mother, Julia. Finn didn't really care if she missed the call. Her mother had decided to leave. It wasn't Finn's job to bend her schedule so Julia felt like she was doing her parental duty.

"I'll try to get home," she lied.

"Are you okay, sweetheart?" Nana covered the few feet between them and raised her hand to touch Finn's forehead. Finn's health and emotional well-being was a subject of constant discussion. She couldn't sneeze without someone asking how she was. Finn was adept at faking a smile and telling people she was fine.

"I'm fine, Nana."

"You look tired."

Even if last night's dream was unsettling—seeing Noah with his eyes open, his plea for help—Finn couldn't think of any reason to tell Nana about it. Nana had lost her son; her grandson was in a coma. What good would extra worry do her? "Just homework. I've been busy."

Nana didn't look convinced, so Finn opened her eyes a little wider, a tip she'd learned on the Internet for convincing people you were telling the truth. It worked. After a moment, Nana reached out and patted Finn's arm. "Make sure Noah eats a good breakfast."

Winter seemed intent on pushing fall out early, and Finn wished she'd put on a coat for the walk to school. With no mountains or forests to block its path, the wind could change the weather from balmy to freezing in an instant.

She stopped outside a two-story wood house with a beautiful wraparound porch. The front yard was covered in brown leaves. Someone had pushed a wheelbarrow full of wood chips to the maple tree that towered over the property. A shovel was sticking out of the pile, evidence of a chore abandoned.

Finn pulled out her phone and typed: *Outside. Cold. Bring me coat. Plz.*

Normally, Jed appeared a millisecond after she texted, but she knew a request for a coat would throw him. Jed had been wearing the same navy-blue hoodie since second grade. Well, not the same one, but the same style. "It makes getting dressed easy," he always said. "Everything goes with blue, especially when you only wear jeans."

She and Jed had been friends since her family had moved here when she was six. Finn vaguely remembered life before, a big city with lots of stuff to do. Her mom worked in a tall office building, and Finn would go to work with her sometimes. She'd stand at the window and wonder how far away the horizon was. But her dad wanted to live someplace smaller, simpler, so they'd moved here.

She'd met Jed that first day. He was riding his bike to get gum at the local convenience store. He stopped to give her a piece on his way home. They'd started walking to school together the next day and hadn't stopped since.

When Noah fell into the coma, everyone at school asked how he was doing. Most of the time, Finn pretended she didn't hear them until they stopped asking. Eventually they all left her alone. Not Jed. He refused to be pushed away.

When she stopped texting him to say she was on the way to school, she'd find him waiting outside for her. When she stopped talking about how Noah was doing, Jed came to her house and sat with Noah himself. When she decided smoking was the answer, he told her she was an idiot and lent her his hoodie so Nana wouldn't smell smoke on her coat and ground her forever. Two weeks later when she realized he was right, she was an idiot for smoking, he didn't say a word. Sometimes Finn felt like Jed was the only thing that kept her from disappearing completely.

The front door opened. Jed held up two coats: one plaid and extra large; the other one a perfectly sized, unattractive teal.

"Which one?" he called out.

"Not to be ungrateful, but are those my only choices?"

"These were the ones I found."

"Did you ask if it was okay if I took them?"

Jed yelled back into the house. "Mom, Finn needs a coat."

Finn heard Jed's mom's voice but not what she was saying. It was like a short melody being played in a far-off room.

"She says you can take whatever you want. I say these are your choices."

"Teal."

Jed tossed the plaid coat inside and picked up his backpack. "Bye!" he shouted back into the house, and closed the door. As he jogged down the sidewalk toward her, Finn noticed that Jed was taller and broader than he'd been this summer. He looked less like the freckled boy from second grade and more like his father, a handsome man with a kind face.

"I couldn't do any of the math problems," he announced when he reached her.

"Did you try?"

Jed was easily distracted, always drawn to the cool thing he hadn't tried yet. As if to drive the point home, he said, "I sat with a pencil, looking at the problems, if that's what you mean. But I was listening to this online radio station from Detroit." He pulled out his phone and slid a finger across the screen. "I heard this song. It'd be your life story if you'd grown up in a project somewhere on the East Coast."

"Which I didn't."

"No, but your dad's dead and your mom took a job half a

planet away for the pay and benefits. As a result, you're alienated and cynical." He hit the screen. "I just sent it to you."

"I'm not alienated."

"So you're admitting to cynical?"

"I look back at cynical from where I'm standing," she said.
Jed laughed.

They separated in the front hallway of school, with a promise
to meet up at lunch.

Finn walked down the hall, staring at the floor. If you aren't
exceptional in some way—or if you made people uncomfort-
able because your brother was in a coma—the best way to go
through high school, Finn had decided, was head down. The
steady banging of lockers made her think it was almost time for
the first-period bell.

Out of the corner of her eye, she saw Deborah Marks—
according to Jed the "most beautiful girl at the school under
five foot four"—talking to Marcus Hahn, the quarterback of
the football team.

Finn and Deborah had been friends in eighth grade. A
momentary overlap of interest in romance literature sparked
a year's worth of lunches comparing novels from *Jane Eyre* to
Twilight. Finn had existed in the halo of Deborah's popular-
ity until high school. It was a fork in the road. Finn went left,
toward fewer friends, more classes, and a personal identity
dominated by tragedy. Deborah, well, she went right, toward
complete school domination. She got respectable grades,

participated in a thousand activities, and was decent to everyone. You wanted to dislike her on principle; it just wasn't easy to do.

Finn glanced over, took in Deborah's outfit: a short skirt with a geometric pattern and a sweater that had an equally busy but competing design. The two things should not go together, but, somehow, they did. Perfectly. Marcus was standing so close they might have been superglued together. Maybe what Jed said the other day was true, that Deborah had broken up with her crosstown boyfriend. That would clear the way for her and Marcus to be together, which they totally should be because they were perfect for each—

Finn's foot caught the leg of a classmate who had kneeled to tie his shoe. She barely kept herself from doing a total faceplant.

"You okay, Finn?" Deborah called over. Finn turned and looked at her. Deborah's face showed only kindness and concern.

Finn sprang up. "I'm fine." She hurried toward her locker. Screw Deborah Marks.

Finn's first class was New World History, which also happened to be her least favorite. Mr. Newsome would give the most boring teacher who'd ever lived a run for his money. And, since he saw the world entirely through a white-male lens, she was learning a lot about "forefathers," but not much about the people they were forefathering over.

Today he was droning on about the House of Stuarts, the

first family to rule over the whole of the United Kingdom. Potentially interesting stuff. The Stuarts, already the rulers of Scotland, take over the British throne, failing to realize the autocratic style they'd practiced in Scotland wouldn't be well received by their new subjects. They almost destroyed the kingdom. It was standard dinner-table talk when Finn was growing up; her father took a lot of pride in their heritage. They were Anglo-Celtic on both sides for a million and one years, or so he used to say.

Mr. Newsome, on the other hand, never talked about any of the good parts of this history, and today was no exception. He was just laying out an array of facts: who lived when; who died where. Thank God she sat in the back so he couldn't see that she hadn't used her pencil for anything other than to write a note to take home her smelly gym clothes.

She glanced across the aisle at "Moby" Dawson, who hadn't once looked up from a drawing in his notebook. It was an intricate cityscape, a spread of buildings that looked more like jails than places people would go voluntarily. Finn wondered how long he'd been working on it.

She didn't know much about Moby. He'd moved to town last summer right before school started. He'd gotten his nickname after building a raft that fell apart as soon as it hit the middle of the river. All the pieces of the raft, and then Moby himself, floated by an "end of summer" barbecue some kids were having. They fished him out, but maybe he wished they hadn't. Because now he was known by the name of a giant white whale. Jed said Moby was a computer genius and could hack into the school's system and change anyone's grades. Finn had never spoken more than five words to him.

In the front of the classroom, Mr. Newsome picked up a pointer and turned to the European map that hung behind him. "Alan fitz Flaad is the oldest known member of the Stuart clan. He was from Breton." Mr. Newsome pointed at France.

Finn stopped listening.

She couldn't get last night's dream out of her head. She'd always envied people who remembered their dreams. This one just reminded her of how much she missed her brother and how utterly helpless she was to save him.

Finn closed her eyes, and the dream spilled back into her mind.

Noah bobbing in the water. His eyes open, scared. "Finn! Help me. Please."

The kelp wrapped around him like a web. And in it, something she hadn't noticed last night, something small, wriggling up through the tangled pieces. Something red and yellow and green.

"Come find me, Finn," Noah said.

What?

Noah hadn't said that last night. Before she could respond, the red-yellow-and-green object burst free, flying right toward Finn as Noah was seized by threads of inky darkness that grabbed him from below. She watched, helplessly, as he was pulled into the depths.

"No!" Finn screamed.

She heard a loud CRACK and—

Her eyes opened.

Moby Dawson and a few of her classmates were staring at her. After a moment, everyone turned away, except for Moby. "You're bleeding," he whispered, pointing at her hand. She looked. She'd snapped her pencil in half. There was blood on her finger where the jagged edge of the pencil had cut her. "Shouldn't hold on so tight," he offered, smiling. Finn forced herself to smile back, but her heart was pounding.

What was going on?

TWO

Finn sat by Noah's bed, Eddie's head resting on her foot. She was supposed to be calculating the area under a curve, but she couldn't focus. Instead, she watched her brother. His breathing seemed ragged. She put a hand on his forehead. He was definitely warm. She stuffed her pad of paper into the textbook and slammed it shut. Her math grade was headed for the toilet, no doubt about it. Without Noah, she was barely hanging on.

The last conversation they'd had was because she'd needed his help. She was stuck on a practice problem and went to find him, walking through his open bedroom door without knocking. He got angry, and she almost left but forced herself to stay. *Remember The Plan,* she'd told herself.

Finn had realized a long time ago that high school wasn't for people like her. She was ordinary and loved simple things: books, long walks . . . pudding. High school was teenagers vying for glory. Finn was the background all those stars moved in front of, like a night sky during a meteor shower. So The Plan was to endure high school and escape to a small liberal-arts college where she'd meet other quiet people trying to figure out who they were and what they wanted.

Swarthmore was her first choice.

But to get there, she needed great grades, and to get those, she needed Noah. So that night, she let him yell at her and then apologized profusely. When that didn't work, she offered to bake him a batch of oatmeal-chocolate-chip cookies. Deal. It took him five minutes to figure out the problem and twenty minutes for her to understand his explanation.

When she stood to leave, he stopped her.

"Besides water," he asked, "what are you afraid of?"

"You writing something for school?"

"No. I'm just wondering."

"That's very profound."

"Yeah, that's me. Profound. So what is it? What are you afraid of?"

"Having to go to my safety school."

"That's not going to happen."

"Still," Finn said. "It's what keeps me up at night." It was clear from the look on his face that her answer was disappointing. "What about you? Other than spiders, what are you afraid of?"

It took Noah a long time to answer.

"Not knowing," he finally said.

"Not knowing what?"

"I don't know. Maybe everything."

"That's way deeper than my safety school answer, but it feels like a recipe for a lifetime of unhappiness."

That night, she'd gone to Jed's for dinner. His mom was making fried chicken, which was Finn's favorite. Noah was asleep when she got home. The next morning, he was in a coma.

Finn knew she'd missed something in that conversation. But no matter how many times she replayed it, she never knew what it was.

Finn crossed the backyard toward the shed where Nana grew the herbs for her home remedies. She opened the door and was overwhelmed by the smell, a mix of grass and flowers and general herbal-ness. As if all of nature were crammed into that tiny room.

Nana turned around from the stone bowl where she was pounding together an aggressively green poultice. Finn recognized it as the one she used on Noah's skin to stave off bedsores. "I thought you had a study group."

"No one was prepared, so we put it off until tomorrow."

"Are you spending too much time talking to Noah and not enough time doing your work? He and I will both understand if you need a different study location."

"I'd miss him. Did you notice his breathing doesn't seem quite right?"

"I did. I spoke to the nurse. She's going to come earlier in the morning." Nana smiled at her. "You're a good sister."

"I wish I could do more than monitor his breathing."

"That's more than what you should have to do."

Nana never left after Noah lapsed into his coma, because Julia had taken her new job. Nana didn't try to parent Finn, but she also didn't ignore her. It was like Nana was always holding a finger up, checking to see which way the wind was blowing. Some days, Finn got a lot of attention; other days, she didn't. Nana didn't pry, so Finn wasn't exactly sure how she knew when Finn was down, but she always did. And then there would be some extra bit of kindness, a freshly baked cake or newly washed favorite sweatshirt. When Finn had to stay home from school with a cold or stomach bug, Nana would sit with her, reading aloud from some old book, her faint Irish accent making the words roll musically into one another.

Nana had been one of the things Finn had missed when they moved out of the city. Her brother's being in a coma was a hard price to pay for getting Nana back.

Nana scraped the poultice into a smaller bowl. "Should we call your mom?"

There was no avoiding it. "I'll get my computer." Finn headed out of the shed, feeling Nana's eyes on her back as she walked away.

Finn set the computer on the tray above Noah's bed, and she and Nana sat quietly, waiting for Julia to pick up. Nana pointed to the cut on Finn's hand.

"What happened?"

The cut looked angry around the edges.

"Faulty pencil." And then, because that sounded ridiculous, she added, "It broke in my hand."

Nana turned and headed to the kitchen right before the familiar beep of the video connection being completed. On the computer, Finn saw her mom sitting in her apartment in front of the large picture window. She lived high above Oslo, and when she called during the day, you could see mountains and fjords in the distance. But it was winter and very late. Tonight, all you could see was black.

"Hi, sweetheart. You look tired."

"Did Nana tell you to say that?" It came out with more attitude than Finn had intended.

"Why would Nana tell me to say that?"

Nana walked back into the room, the bowl of green goo in her hand. "Because I said the same thing this morning." She looked at Finn. "So could be it's true." Nana picked up Finn's hand and rubbed the poultice on her wound.

"Margaret," her mother asked, "is she getting enough sleep?"

Nana spun the computer around so she was on camera. "Don't worry, Julia. I'll make sure she does." When Finn spun the computer back, her mom had a worried look on her face; when she saw Finn, she covered it with a smile.

"How's Noah doing?" she asked.

Finn glanced at her grandmother, who looked away.

Finn's grandmother was old-school. She grew up on a farm,

way out in the country. She subscribed to a "know your neighbor, help your neighbor" way of life and was the most open and loving person Finn had ever known. Finn couldn't remember Nana ever averting her eyes from someone.

"Finn? How's Noah?" her mother repeated.

Finn forced herself to pay attention. "Good. All things considered." She centered the camera on Noah. There was a long moment as Julia took in her sleeping son.

"Hi, honey. You would have loved the boat trip I took yesterday. Six hours on calm seas to the platform. I saw a pod of whales."

There was a pause. Finn wasn't watching the screen, but she knew her mother was doing what she always did.

Waiting . . . hoping Noah would respond.

Finn and her grandmother sat at the kitchen table over a dinner of chicken in gravy with green beans and homemade bread. It was delicious, but Finn couldn't bring herself to finish what was on her plate.

"So are you going to tell me?" Nana asked.

"Tell you what?"

"What's going on. I see it. The wheels are spinning."

Finn shook her head. "It's nothing."

"Sweetheart, we're family. It doesn't have to be something. If your socks are too scratchy or your toothpaste's too minty, I want to hear about it."

Finn knew that if she didn't tell Nana what was going on,

Nana would ask again. And again. Not with any malice, just with love and concern, so she could figure out how to help. It was impossible to resist, and Finn knew that, eventually, she would tell Nana the truth. Why delay the inevitable?

"I don't usually remember my dreams, but last night I did. It's made me . . . jumpy."

Nana carried her half-finished dinner to the garbage can. She scraped it into the trash. "What was the dream about?" She asked so quietly that Finn barely heard her.

"I was on an ice sheet, but for some reason I was really hot." Finn stopped, hoping that would end the conversation. But Nana waited for her to go on. "I melted through the ice and into the ocean and . . . Noah was there. He woke up and said he needed help."

Her grandmother came and sat down in the chair next to her. She took one of Finn's hands. "No wonder you're sad."

"I can't get it out of my head. At school today, I even fell asleep and dreamed the whole thing again."

"So maybe I'm right, and you're tired."

Finn smiled as she moved the food around on her plate. "You've been right before, Nana. I suppose it's possible."

"It must have been hard to see Noah," Nana said. It was, but Finn wasn't ready to talk about it, so she stayed silent. Nana let it pass. "You know," she said. "They say that in your dreams all the people are you."

"And if I'm Noah, what's that mean?"

Nana leaned to kiss Finn on the head. "I don't know. It's

just something I've heard. I'll make you some tea to help you sleep tonight."

Finn stood and picked up her plate to clean it off. Nana took it. "I'll clean up. You start your homework."

Finn headed toward her room. Something made her turn around. She saw her grandmother, phone in her hand, headed out the back door.

Finn turned to the next page in *Fahrenheit 451*. The line ". . . with nothing to say" was at the top, staring back at her. She realized she couldn't remember the beginning of the sentence from the previous page. In fact, she couldn't remember anything that had happened in this chapter. She set the book facedown on her nightstand and tucked her pencil into the pocket of her shirt so she'd remember to sharpen it. The English assignment would have to wait. Thank God the paper wasn't due until next week.

Finn looked around at the pale-yellow walls of her bedroom.

Her parents had always been cool about letting Finn and Noah decorate their bedrooms. Finn picked a pale yellow to use as a background for her constantly changing collections: A photo of a vast desert landscape she ripped from a magazine would replace a takeout menu that had made her laugh because of the crazy misspellings; the picture she and Jed had co-drawn during lunch would replace the jacket from one of her father's vinyl records.

As she looked around now, it struck her that since Noah's coma she hadn't changed anything. The room was stuck. She was stuck. They were all stuck.

There was a knock. "Come in."

Her grandmother opened the door, and Eddie padded into the room and jumped up onto Finn's bed.

"I made you tea."

"How bad does it taste?"

"I added some honey."

"To sweeten the bad taste?"

Nana set the mug on the side table. Finn could tell she had something to say.

"I'm not going to lapse into a coma, Nana." Nana blinked hard, and Finn immediately regretted the words. "That was a joke. Sorry, I know it wasn't funny."

Nana sat down on the bed. "In your dream last night," she asked, "how did Noah look?"

Finn watched Nana age in an instant, and she suddenly realized just how hard this must be for her. She was with Noah all day. She sat at his bedside while Finn was at school. She probably talked to him. It must feel so sad and lonely.

"He looked good," Finn said, ignoring the memory of his pale skin and limp body. "Remember how blue his eyes are?"

Nana nodded.

"I didn't get that good of a look before I started drowning," Finn continued, trying to find a path out of the lie. "You know me and water."

"It's never too late to take lessons, sweetheart."

"So I can swim in big lakes filled with slimy creatures. No thank you."

Her grandmother reached out and tucked a stray piece of hair behind Finn's ear.

"You can swim in a pool."

"Or I could just avoid water for the rest of my life."

"Or you could do that."

Nana kissed her on the forehead and headed out of the room, leaving the door open so Eddie could find his way back to Noah when he was ready. Finn reached for the mug and brought it to her nose. "It smells like garbage," she said to the dog. "Honey-glazed garbage."

But she'd rather sleep through the night than drown in her dreams, so Finn held her nose and took a sip. It was wet sand on her tongue. She drank it quickly and then held the empty mug out for Eddie to see. He must have been satisfied, because he jumped off the bed and headed toward Noah's room.

I should change out of my clothes, Finn thought. She lay down instead. It took only an instant before she was asleep.

It was dark.

Finn put her hand out and hit a wall. She turned around, arms extended, and took another step. Almost immediately, she felt another wall. She reached out all around her. She was standing in a space no more than four feet wide.

She ran her hands down her body, felt her jeans and T-shirt, the clothes she'd fallen asleep in. And in the pocket of her shirt, the pencil she'd tucked into it. She pulled it out and banged it against the wall. She reached out and touched the spot to feel if she'd made a dent. Yes. She hit the wall again.

And again.

And again.

The pencil broke but not before it made a small hole. A shaft of flickering light pierced the dark space, bringing with it a cacophony of muffled sounds.

She pressed her eye to the hole. She saw . . . what? Finn didn't know. It was like movies, or pieces of movies, images, but flying by so fast.

People: running, walking, falling, kissing, chasing, and being chased.

Monsters and storms.

Alien worlds, fire, water.

Every color imaginable.

Flowing over and around the room where she was. Rushing toward her and away. As if she were in the middle of a river, a fast-moving river of . . .

She must be having a dream. But she'd never been aware of having a dream before. There was a name for that, wasn't there . . . ? Lucid dream. This was so strange, as though her dream had dropped into everyone else's.

A woman on a large purple butterfly glanced in Finn's direction just as a noxious odor, like rotten eggs or a thousand blown-out matches, blew into the tiny room.

Finn pushed down the feeling of nausea the smell caused. "Hey!" she called as the woman sped by. "Over—"

The rest of the sentence died in her throat.

Her father, Conor, was standing right in front of her.

Not dead, strapped in an airplane seat at the bottom of a lake. But right there on the other side of the wall, unaffected by the flow around him. The images, the movies, moved away from him, almost like they were repelled by his presence. Finn saw him lean to look through the hole. She stepped back so he could see her. "Daddy, it's me, Finn."

But before he could see her, something pale shoved him aside. Finn rushed forward and looked through the hole to see what was happening. Conor was a few feet away, unharmed, looking at—

Noah.

Barely more than a wisp of smoke. Noah was screaming at him, but no sounds came out of his mouth. Noah, or what there was of him, rushed at his father again. Conor flicked his hand. Noah broke apart, the pieces of him spinning away as if they'd been caught in a gust of wind. Finn watched them disappear.

"Noah!" Finn screamed.

She looked back at her father. Conor leaned in, but this time, he just covered the hole with his hand. The smell, the sulfurous smell became overwhelming. And then, a buzzing sound filled the room. Her head pounded as though something was trying to get inside it. She covered her ears and slid to the ground, trying to keep it—whatever it was—out. Her brain felt like it was on fire.

She wanted the buzzing to stop; she wanted everything to be quiet. She tried to think of something, anything, other than the pain.

Her favorite sweatshirt popped into her head. The one she'd dropped in last night's dream. How soft it was. Fit just right. And the words on the front. Emily Dickinson. Hope. Feathers. It's a bird, Finn thought.

The buzzing stopped. The horrible smell was gone.

Her head throbbing, Finn stood up and looked through the small hole in the wall.

Her father was nowhere to be seen.

THREE

"You're ten minutes late and I'm freezing," Jed called out from fifty feet away.

Finn checked her watch. He was right. She'd left her house on time. Being tired had really slowed her down.

The dream had continued last night, though her father never returned and neither did Noah. Finn was left to wrestle with all her questions alone. Why didn't her father help her? What made Noah attack him? Why was she in that box? And what was all that stuff outside?

She'd watched the "movies" until she'd finally gotten so tired, she curled up in a ball on the floor and closed her eyes. The next thing she knew, her alarm was going off.

"You should have left without me," she told Jed.

"And deny myself the chance to tell you that I finished the biology problem set *and* got a date for the winter dance."

"I'm impressed. I didn't know you'd gotten up the courage to talk to Aileen, let alone ask her to the dance."

"It's not Aileen."

"You love Aileen."

"I don't love her. I think she's beautiful. But there's not a chance in hell that she'll go out with me. Besides, is her mom really going to let her go to the winter dance?"

"Probably not. So who is it?"

"You." Finn looked at him sideways. "Remember our pact? If we were thirty and unmarried, we'd get hitched?"

"Yes. We're not thirty. And a dance is not a marriage."

"No, but since we've known each other, there have been thirty-one dances. Two each year of middle school equals four. Five freshman year. That's nine. None this year, but two each year at the tennis club since second grade, that's another sixteen and gets us to twenty-five."

"I'm not marrying you when I'm twenty-five."

"Six dance lessons when we were nine. That's thirty-one. I haven't had a date to any of them. So, in the spirit of our pact, you should go with me."

"How late were you up figuring this out?"

"Come on, Finn. I want to go to the dance, and I don't want to go alone."

Finn knew there were at least a half dozen girls at school who were dying for Jed to ask them to the dance. He just hadn't noticed.

"It's one night," he continued. "And we'll leave early if it's painful." Finn wasn't in the mood to go to the dance, but Jed was her best friend, and she didn't take his loyalty lightly.

"Can I think about it?"

"You know you're going to say yes."

"Then give me a day or two so I can pretend I'm making my own decision."

"Take all the time you need." He grabbed the backpack off her shoulder. Finn had long since stopped trying to convince him she could carry her own bag. The truth was it weighed a ton and the chances of her tripping on the sidewalk were a lot greater if she wore it. She was willing to sacrifice her independence if it meant she'd have fewer bruises.

Marcus Hahn was already sitting at their table with his lab book open when Finn entered biology class. It struck her as odd. Marcus was plenty smart, but he didn't seem motivated to do any better than he needed to in order to get a football scholarship to college. When she sat down, she saw he was drawing X's and O's, which she knew were football plays because one of the few times she'd talked to him about something other than biology she'd asked him about it.

"Hi, Marcus," she said quietly as she slid onto her stool. He didn't look up.

"Hey, Phineas," Marcus responded. She liked this nickname even less than her real name, but she'd never had the nerve to tell him.

"Isn't football season over?" He didn't answer, just closed his lab book. They sat in silence while other students filed into the room. "I didn't mean to make you stop," Finn said, gesturing toward his book. "I was just asking. I really don't know if football season is over."

"We lost in the sectionals two weeks ago."

"Oh. Sorry." She should just stop talking. She should just face the front of the classroom and wait for Mrs. Reynolds to start class. Today, for some reason, she couldn't.

"You love football, don't you?"

Marcus looked at her like she was crazy. "What?"

"That came out stupid. What I mean is, the season's over, you lost, yet here you are . . ." She pointed at his lab book. "I'm not sure what you call it."

"Diagramming plays."

"You're sitting here diagramming plays, presumably for future football games. Which I guess means that you care about football more than I care about any nonliving thing in my life. And that's good for you and not so good for me." Marcus looked at her blankly. "Maybe it just means I need a hobby," she said.

Mrs. Reynolds stepped to the front of the class and wrote *The Limbic System* on the whiteboard. Marcus turned away, and Finn opened her lab book. *Marcus Hahn*, she thought, *will definitely not be inviting me to the winter dance.*

Finn carried her tray toward Jed, who'd found an empty table near the windows.

"An apple and three packs of saltines?" he said as she sat down. "That's a sad lunch. This spaghetti, on the other hand, is amazing. It's crunchy and soggy all at the same time."

"I'm not hungry."

"What's going on with you?"

"Nothing."

"You are so lying. And I know that because one of the many things I admire about you is your appetite. But you're not eating today, and you didn't eat yesterday. And you've got these huge, dark . . ." He made a gesture near her face. "Circles." He stopped gesturing and took another bite of spaghetti.

"I'm not sleeping well." Finn needed to talk to someone. "I'm having horrible dreams. Last night, it was my dad. He kept me trapped in a tiny room while all these weird images streamed by outside. The night before, it was Noah, and he was wrapped in kelp and needed my help. Of course, the dream was underwater. You know how much I love water." She cut a piece out of her apple. "My whole life, I've remembered one or two dreams total. Now, I've remembered two in two nights, and they both suck."

Jed took another bite of pasta. Chewed it thoughtfully.

"It is true that you hate water," he said after he swallowed. "But that seems a little transparent as dreams go, so I'm going to say the water's about your mom, who happens to be an expert on the stuff. You miss your brother, so you'd totally want to help him. And your father was a great guy who died tragically, putting your real-life hopes, at least temporarily, on hold. Put it all together and you've got some easy-to-translate dreams about the really sad things that have happened to you and your family. Hence that song I sent you. Did you listen to it?"

"Not yet. You think these dreams are all about my family?"

"Was Nana in them?"

"Nope."

"Which makes sense because she is totally cool and doesn't deserve to be trashed by your subconscious."

Finn smiled, watching as he took another bite of his spaghetti. "I've got to say, Jed, your lunch looks disgusting."

"Yeah, crunchy and soggy is totally gross. You just seemed down, so I was trying to be positive." And with that, he took another bite.

When Finn got home, Nana was sitting in the living room with Rafe Newell. "Finn," Rafe said. "You've had a growth spurt." He attempted a smile, but it made him look more like a snake than a human being.

Noah had studied martial arts with Rafe for a year before he went into the coma, but Finn hadn't met him until afterward. When she did finally meet him, she had two strong feelings: a desire to freeze, followed by the instinct to flee. It might have been his sheer size. Rafe was at least six and a half feet tall and solid. Finn's mom used to say some babies had "bones made of lead." Rafe Newell seemed like a man made of lead. And, even though she knew her brother loved him, he made Finn uneasy.

She wanted to keep moving through the room but knew Nana wouldn't allow it. So she stood by the arm of the couch and said, "Hello, Rafe," with as little enthusiasm as she thought she could get away with.

"How is school?"

"Good." Short and sweet was all he was going to get from her.

Rafe dropped his smile. His regular face wasn't any more comforting than his not-so-friendly smile. "Well, good to see you," she lied. "I'm just going to grab a snack and start my homework."

"Don't be rude, Finn. Rafe came to visit both of us."

Nana's tone made it clear Finn didn't have a choice, so she moved to the only spot available, the one on the couch near Rafe. As she sat down, Rafe reached for a necklace on the coffee table. At least, it looked like a necklace. It was a small yellow crystal on a shiny silver chain.

"Your grandmother tells me you've been having a hard time sleeping."

Finn shot Nana a look. She had no business telling Rafe anything.

"I remember when I was about your age, my dream life suddenly seemed very . . . real. Made my sleep a little unsettled." She could feel him staring at her, even though her back was to him. "Is that what it feels like to you?"

Finn didn't care how much her brother liked Rafe. She was not going to open up to him. She turned back to him, ready to shut the conversation down, but he wasn't looking at her. He was staring at the crystal on the chain. She followed his eyes.

The charm . . . was straining to reach her, pulling the chain parallel to the floor. She started to say something, ask him how he was doing the trick, because it had to be a trick. But before she could, Rafe took the chain in his still-gloved left hand. The crystal collapsed, and the chain went limp. He dropped them both into a velvet bag.

"It looks like Finn is already focused on what she needs to do tonight, Margaret. Maybe we should let her get to it."

Finn wanted to get away from Rafe, his questions, his weird necklace. She turned to her grandmother. "Can I go, Nana? Is that okay?" When her grandmother didn't answer, Finn reached out and touched her arm. "Nana?"

Rafe stood up. "I could use a glass of water."

Nana forced a smile on her face. "Will you get him some, Finn?"

Spending any longer with Rafe was the last thing Finn wanted to do, but she led him into the kitchen and poured him a glass. He drank it in one swallow before quickly glancing into Noah's room. "I sure do miss him," Rafe said. And then, without waiting for Finn's response, he headed back to where her grandmother sat waiting.

From her perch by Noah's bed, she could hear bits and pieces of their conversation. It sounded like Rafe was pushing Nana to do something she didn't want to do, and then, after a few minutes, Finn heard the front door open and close.

She forced herself to focus on her limbic system science homework. If she finished it, she'd have only *Fahrenheit 451* and some history to do tonight. It would take a couple of hours, tops. Then she could go to bed, hopefully get a good night's sleep.

"Finn, could you come here?" Nana called from the kitchen.

Finn found her grandmother sitting at the table, her hands resting on a blue spiral notebook. Finn checked her phone. It was dinnertime. "Nana, you look tired. Why don't I call and get us a pizza?"

Nana pushed the notebook toward her. "I think you should look at this."

"What is it?"

"Noah's notebook."

"Noah kept a journal?" Finn had a hard time imagining her brother, a guy who loved Mountain Dew and video games, writing in a journal.

Finn opened the notebook. It wasn't what she expected. Instead of dated entries about school or girls or his favorite video game character, it was page after page of drawings and precise, almost manic, notations. Some drawings looked like maps. Others were monstrous creatures you'd find in fantasy novels. People were drawn as stick figures running, flying, fighting, dying. They reminded her of the movies she'd seen in her dream last night. And around all of it, there were lists: words, names, and dates, with arrows connecting one thing to the next.

"Why are you showing me this?" Finn asked.

"Rafe thinks it's important."

Finn resented Rafe's involvement, but she ignored the snide comment that popped into her mind and flipped through the rest of the notebook quickly until she got to the last page. Noah had drawn a maze. He'd put waves above it to show it was underwater.

The maze had two openings, one at the top and the other at

the bottom. At the maze's center, there was a symbol: a triangle inside a circle in the middle of a square. At the top of the page, there was a drawing of a hummingbird. Noah had labeled the body red, the wings yellow, and the head green. It looked . . . fierce, unlike any hummingbird Finn had seen in real life.

She'd seen it before.

In her dream at school.

The tangle of kelp around her brother. Something struggling to burst free.

The flash of red, yellow, green.

It was a hummingbird. Fierce, not friendly. Just like the one Noah drew.

She pushed the notebook away.

"What is it, Finn?"

Her chest felt tight. She couldn't breathe. Her mind was blank, and it took a minute to remember where she was.

In the kitchen.

Talking to Nana . . . about . . . ?

What?

Noah.

"Finn, what's going on?"

Why were the images from that dream stalking her? And how could Noah's drawings, which she'd never seen, end up in her head? Finn saw the concern in Nana's eyes. Obviously, there had been something wrong with Noah. Was there something wrong with her, too? She shook off the fear that was pressing at the edges of her mind. There had to be an explanation, but it took a moment for her to think of something that made any sense at all. Nana waited until finally Finn said, "Did you know that after Dad died, Noah thought he came back as a hummingbird?"

Nana shook her head. "No. I didn't."

"Noah would sit for hours in the yard or down at the park. Not doing anything, just sitting. We thought he was sad and left him alone. And then one night, Mom sent me to get him for dinner. He told me he wasn't ready to come in. That he and Dad weren't finished."

Finn remembered it like it was yesterday. Six-year-old Noah had taken her hand and walked her toward the honeysuckle bush at the back of the yard. As they got closer, a hummingbird launched itself into the early-evening sky. Until that instant, Finn hadn't known those whistling sounds she heard sometimes were hummingbirds taking flight.

When they couldn't see the bird anymore, Noah turned to Finn and said, "Dad's a hummingbird. He comes back to me all the time." The way he had said it, it was as though their father's being a bird was the most normal thing in the world. And here it was again all these years later. A hummingbird.

"All this stuff in the notebook. Maybe . . . Noah never got over Dad dying."

"This isn't grief, Finn. These are dreams. Other people's dreams. Your brother had a . . . gift. He was like a shaman. He could go into other people's dreams and help them. They're called Dreamwalkers. Your brother was a Dreamwalker."

Finn looked at her grandmother, trying to figure out what the joke was, but Nana looked completely serious. Finn headed to the stove. "Why don't I make you some tea?"

She turned on the flame under the kettle. Behind her, Finn heard Nana stand up and walk to the living room. She came back with the Driscoll family tree that hung over the piano. Ending with Finn's great-grandfather Patrick, it traced the family back twenty generations. Nana set it on the counter. "See how some of them are framed in clouds?" She looked at Finn to make sure she was paying attention. "They are the known Driscoll family Dreamwalkers. For more than six hundred years, at least one per generation. Twenty-two boys and girls, revealed around their sixteenth birthdays."

"Nana, I don't know what you expect me to say, but—"

"I'm not making this up, Finn. Look at the notebook."

Finn pointed to the open page. "It seems crazy."

"You saw Noah, Finn. Every day. You talked to him. Did he seem crazy? Like anything was wrong with him?"

No. In the months before his coma, Noah was calm, confident. Alive.

"These are dreams, Finn. Other people's dreams. Your brother had the gift, or the curse. At this point, it's hard to know."

The kettle started to whistle. Finn turned the burner off and looked at the notebook. She stared at a drawing of a small man dwarfed by a spiky-headed monster. It looked like something from a horror movie or nightmare. Still . . . how could what Nana was saying be true?

"Noah was only fourteen when he started showing the signs. Much younger than the others," Nana said, talking so quietly that Finn had to lean forward to hear her clearly. "I did everything I could to keep him from realizing what was happening and acting on it. But it didn't work. We couldn't stop him. Noah wouldn't let us."

"Who's 'we'?"

"Your mother and me."

Everyone in the family knew but her? No way. "Nana, if this was going on, Noah would've told me."

"We asked him not to."

"Why?"

"We thought it was best. Until his training was complete."

It clicked. "Rafe trained him."

Her grandmother must have heard the judgment in her voice because she immediately said, "*Someone* had to. Rafe is a Dreamwalker. Family members in Ireland, other Dreamwalkers, helped me find him. He didn't want to train Noah, but he eventually agreed. We all just wanted Noah to be . . . safe."

A wave of anger and confusion crashed over Finn.

"Is this why Noah's sick?"

"I don't know why Noah's sick."

"Don't bullshit me, Nana. Why is Noah in a coma?"

"I don't know." Nana took a deep breath, used it to steady

herself. Finn realized her grandmother was scared. "But now . . . Rafe thinks Noah's reaching out to you for help. He thinks you're a Dreamwalker, too."

Finn crossed to the kitchen table and sat down.

Nana lowered herself into the chair across the table. They were silent until Finn finally said, "Noah was in my dream last night."

"You had a dream last night?"

Finn nodded and told Nana about it.

"Didn't you drink the tea?"

"Yeah, I did. Why?"

"It was supposed to help you have a dreamless sleep."

"Didn't work."

"It didn't work for Noah, either." Nana looked at her hands for a long moment. "I'm going to call your mother, and then we need to go see Rafe."

"Why do we need to see Rafe?"

"To keep you safe, Finn."

A thousand questions swirled in Finn's mind. She watched Nana start to head toward her bedroom. "Safe from what, Nana? What does a Dreamwalker do?"

Nana stopped. "I don't really know, sweetheart. I mean, I've obviously heard things. About the river, explanations of the powers, the responsibilities. But I'm not sure I really understand it. Rafe can tell you more."

Nana continued down the hall.

After a moment, Finn picked up Noah's notebook and

headed into his room. She laid it on her brother's chest and turned the pages, trying to imagine why he'd written it. At the top of one page, she saw an orange circle. She smiled, imagining Noah eating Cheetos while writing his notes. Finn touched the orange smudge and then flipped to the next page.

That's when she saw it. Next to a childish drawing of a frog using scissors to cut a heart out of a piece of paper, he'd written, *Finn. Crush? Marcus Hahn.*

A memory pushed forward. Biology class, the day they dissected frogs. It was horrible. Finn couldn't make a single incision. Marcus Hahn had done the whole thing. Every time Mrs. Reynolds walked by, Marcus would hand Finn the blade so it looked like she was participating. She'd been so grateful. That night, she'd dreamed about it. The dream stood out because, until the last few days, it was one of the few she'd ever remembered.

But she'd never told Noah about the class. Or the dream. Before he went into the coma, she never told him how she felt about Marcus. She was sure of it. There was no way for him to know, unless . . .

Her heart started racing. What if what Nana said was true? What if . . . Noah could walk through people's dreams? She leaned close to her brother's ear. "If you were spying on me, I will hunt you down and make you pay."

She watched Noah, waiting, hoping for a response. But there wasn't one.

FOUR

Nana's mind was clearly somewhere else as they drove across town. Finn had to remind her to turn on her headlights.

Before they left the house, Finn had gone to her room and typed *Dreamwalker* into a search engine. She mostly got back dream interpretation websites and a few about Native American traditions for finding wisdom in the world of dreams. The most interesting site referred to a tribe in the Northwest that created a map to the afterlife from directions people had received in their dreams. It seemed like a good subject for a history or social sciences paper.

Finn had tried to ask her grandmother some of the questions that were buzzing in her head, mostly about how walking through dreams had caused Noah to lapse into a coma. But Nana didn't know, or just didn't want to say. So Finn stopped asking.

It was cold outside, and the streets were nearly empty. Finn saw only one person, a man in a down coat and fuzzy hat walking a large and ferocious-looking dog.

When they pulled up in front of Joe's Boxing Gym, Nana put the car in park but didn't turn it off. "We don't know how long this will take," she said. "So Rafe will drive you home when you're finished."

"The guy's a douche. I don't want him driving me home."

"Language."

"I don't like him."

The heat was on in the car, but Finn could feel the cold radiating off the window to her door. *Winter's here*, she thought.

"I don't want you to get hurt, Finn. Rafe's the only one I know who can help."

Finn felt a stab of anger in her chest. If it was so dangerous, why did anyone let Noah do it? There must have been a way to stop him. Why hadn't they told Finn so she could help?

"Nana," Finn said, turning toward her grandmother. The light from inside the gym reflected off the tears in Nana's eyes. Nana was crying. Finn suddenly couldn't remember what she was about to say.

"Go inside, Fionnuala. Please."

"Okay," Finn said quietly, and then she climbed out of the car and headed into the gym. Only when Finn was inside the gym did her grandmother put the car in drive and pull away.

The gym smelled like a combination of sweat and herbs, vaguely reminiscent of Nana's shed. Finn looked around but didn't see Rafe, just a few people working out. An older woman viciously punched a hanging bag in the back of the room, like it had stolen her purse and she was going to get even with it, and two young men were doing mixed martial arts in the ring at the center of the gym. Their punches and kicks echoed loudly through the room. Finn winced when one of them took a blow to the head and fell to the ground.

The woman on the heavy bag finally stopped her assault. "You Finn?" she called out.

"Yes."

"Rafe said to tell you he's upstairs."

The woman pointed to the wooden stairs leading to a second floor.

"Thank you," Finn said, but the woman had already returned to her workout, punching with even more fury.

The wooden stairs didn't fit with the rest of the building. There were holes, broken slats, and places where the wood was so thin you could read through it. The stairway looked downright dangerous. Finn glanced around. There didn't appear to be another way up to the second floor.

She put a foot onto the bottom stair. Even though it seemed solid, it sagged under just a little bit of weight. She decided she didn't trust it or the second step and skipped to the third one. She continued like this, making conscious decisions about where to place her feet, until she reached the top. Then she looked at the wooden door in front of her. It was covered with carvings: A river flowed around the outside edge of the door with hundreds, maybe thousands, of people, places, and things hugging its banks. The carving was beautifully intricate and, like the stairs, exhausting.

She raised a hand to knock on the door. "Come in, Finn," Rafe called from inside the room before she'd made contact.

Finn opened the door.

She entered a room that was as calm as the stairs and door were busy. Rafe stood by a table carved from a single piece of wood. The surface was worn smooth and shiny. Bookshelves lined the walls, filled with leather-bound volumes. The ceiling was a color Finn couldn't quite describe except to think that it was incredibly soothing, and the floor . . . Finn had never experienced anything like it. As she walked to the table, her feet sank into it and were then pushed up. As though she was being propelled forward.

Rafe was drinking something out of a brown ceramic mug. Another mug filled with steaming liquid sat across the table.

"I made you some tea," he said.

"I don't like tea."

"While we're going through your training, you don't have a choice, and trust me, it doesn't taste better when it's cold."

Finn sat down but left the tea alone. "What's with the stairs?" she asked.

"I made them myself."

"You miss a lot of classes when you took shop in high school?"

She meant it as a joke, but he clearly didn't think it was funny. He got up and crossed to the center of the room. She watched him fold himself into a seated position on the floor.

"If you've decided to drink it later, then please join me." Finn noticed, and hated, his assumption that she was going to give in and drink the tea.

She stayed put. "Why is my brother in a coma?"

"I don't know."

"Then what makes you think I can help him?"

"I don't know if you can."

He reached into his pocket and pulled out the velvet bag he brought to her house. "This is a Herderite crystal. For thousands of years, it has been used to identify Dreamwalkers. Hundreds of years ago, people used the crystals to find the 'witches' who were letting demons into their dreams." He reached into the bag and grabbed the chain with his bare hand. The minute it was free of the fabric, the crystal shot toward Finn like it had been fired out of a gun. She reacted, startled. But Rafe held tight to the chain so the crystal hung in the air, defying gravity.

"How are you doing that?"

"I'm not. You are. Something about the way Dreamwalkers vibrate." He slipped the velvet bag over the crystal and then let go of it with his bare hand. The tension in the bag disappeared.

Finn desperately wanted to leave, but the memory of the tears in her grandmother's eyes stopped her. If she was stuck, then there was no reason not to learn as much as she could. She crossed to Rafe and sat down on the floor.

"You ever read Jung?" he asked.

Finn shook her head.

"You know anything about the collective unconscious?" Finn shook her head again. "Axis mundi?"

"No."

"What exactly do they teach you in school?"

"How to make stairs that don't kill people."

Finn saw a small smile play at the corners of his mouth, but it quickly faded.

"Most people experience dreams passively, and their dreams, for the most part, are benign: They are a top hat–wearing banana slug or have sex with a favorite rock star. Those dreams are not our concern. Dreamwalkers exist to face the terrors: fears that come from being chased by monsters they can't see and won't fight. When that happens, people call out for help."

Finn noticed that Rafe's left ear was higher than his right and that he'd missed a spot the last time he shaved. He also had a scar, a clean and symmetrical line circling around half his neck. She was wondering about what might have caused it when she realized he wasn't talking anymore. He glared at her a beat before continuing. "Dreamwalkers are the warriors of the unconscious, moving through the dream space to battle the fears people face in their sleep. You help others find peace in their dreams so they can have peace in their lives." His finger traced a wavy pattern on the floor. "Dreamwalkers wade into the River so the world stays in balance."

"This sounds like something you heard on a talk show."

Rafe leaned forward and spoke in barely a whisper. "It's not. And what your grandmother knows and you do not is that the River of Dreams is one of the most powerful forces in the universe. If you don't treat it with respect, the dreams will sweep you away. Or worse, fill you up until there is no you left." He stared at her, clearly daring her to challenge him. She decided not to take the bait.

"Is that what happened to Noah?"

"I don't know."

She thought he was lying. He confirmed the lie by looking away. "Dreamwalkers don't usually come into their power before age sixteen," he finally said. "Obviously, Noah was younger. Maybe he was too young for the fight."

Finn couldn't picture her brother as a warrior. Not because he wasn't strong or brave, but mostly because he never seemed to care about what was going on around him. Like any teenage boy, he often seemed trapped in his own head. Were the names in his notebook people he helped?

"You know, this Dreamwalker thing, how come I've never heard of it? I looked on the Internet, and there's nothing."

"If you go around talking about how you can walk through people's dreams and fight monsters, folks think you're crazy. Probably better to keep it to yourself. At least, that's what most Dreamwalkers decide to do."

This was the first thing he'd said that made any sense.

"Nana says you're a Dreamwalker. Why didn't Noah reach out to you?"

"He can't."

"Why not?"

"It's just not possible," he snapped. "Do you want me to help you or not?"

Finn bit her tongue. Her brain was screaming *run*, but if dealing with Rafe was what it took to find out what happened to her brother, she was willing to do it.

"Yeah, I do," she said.

"Tell me about the dreams you've been having."

Finn gave him an abridged version, and when she finished, he started asking questions.

He wanted details, lots and lots of details: how Noah looked, did he seem to be struggling, where had the hummingbird come from, how had Finn felt, was she able to do anything unusual. After a long series of questions, he stopped and furrowed his brow. "When you were at school," he finally asked. "You were thinking about the first dream and then . . . ?"

"I fell asleep."

"You're sure?"

"Yes."

Finn was tired of his questions. It was time he answered some of hers. "Why did Noah keep getting pulled from me? First like a tornado, then as smoke?"

She could tell he didn't want to answer it, or maybe he didn't like that she'd interrupted him, but he did anyway. "Your brother has gone to a deep, dark place. Something has hold of him. He's fighting, trying to reach you. But the effort would be hard to sustain." Finn thought back to her brother's breathing, how it wasn't as strong today as it had been before. Was what was happening in her dreams affecting Noah in real life?

"In the dream last night," Rafe continued, "was your father wearing a glowing cord anywhere on his body?"

Finn didn't know.

"Think harder. You can remember everything you saw," he said. "That's the difference between you and regular people. Everyone else forgets what they dream. They have to make a conscious effort to remember. You'll have to make a conscious effort to forget."

The way Rafe said it, that didn't seem like a good thing.

"Finn, was your father wearing anything that glowed?" Rafe demanded. "Think about it. Pause the memory if you have to, and look around."

Finn bit her tongue to keep herself from lashing out at him. She was angry. At Rafe, at the situation, but after a minute, she closed her eyes.

For Nana. And Noah. Not for anyone else. After a moment, she was calm enough to bring back the dream. She saw herself—

Trapped in the box as her father approached. In the background, the smoky wisps of Noah were flying away.

Her father wore a high-collared shirt, so she couldn't see his neck. She took a breath and slowed everything down.

Her father. Barely moving. She watched him. She could see the look in his eyes: cold and unfeeling, not at all like the man she remembered. Where was the man who taught her how to ride a bike and throw a baseball, the man who loved to cook hot dogs over an open fire and read books until way past bedtime? Her father had been kind and gentle. At least, that's the way she remembered him.

He'd been dead a long time. Did she remember him wrong? She

knew she was supposed to look for a glowing item. But Finn was
drawn back to his eyes, his cold eyes.

Why was he looking at her like that?

She watched him lift his hand to put it in front of the hole. Why
did he want to block her view?

His eyes . . . so dark.

Why wouldn't he help her; why was he looking at her like that?

"Dad," she whimpered, still caught in the memory. "Dad,
please."

From someplace far away, she heard Rafe talking to her.
"Finn?" She opened her eyes, tried to clear the image from her
head.

"I couldn't see anything that glowed."

"How about you? Were you wearing a necklace or a bracelet? Were you able to see in the dark?"

Finn forced herself to go back into the memory of the
dream.

She saw her hands, reaching through the darkness.

"I could see my hands."

"Then you have one."

"One what?"

"A Lochran. It's the source of your power."

"Like a superhero's cape?"

"Clark Kent wears a suit, but he's still Superman, cape or
no cape. Without your Lochran, you are not a Dreamwalker."

"Why?"

He took a minute and finally just said, "I don't know." It hung there. A moment of truth, better than all his bravado. He stood up. "For some reason, a long, long time ago, the Lochran was gifted to some and not to others. Nobody really knows how or why. But here we are."

He walked to the table. He grabbed the mug of tea and brought it back to her. "This will taste like shit. A hard way to learn to drink it while it's hot. It's not as strong as what your grandmother gave you last night but—"

"She said that tea was just to help me sleep better."

"In a manner of speaking. It was supposed to put you to sleep so deeply you had limited access to the River."

"She drugged me?"

"Just because dreams aren't in this reality doesn't mean they can't hurt you. Something happened to your brother in the dream space, something that kept him from coming back. Your grandmother doesn't want that to happen to you. She did what she thought was best."

Finn looked in the mug at a liquid that looked like dirt mixed with motor oil. She drank it. It tasted like dirt mixed with motor oil.

"Tonight," Rafe said, "you'll have dreams. This tea helps you focus your intentions. When your dream starts, I want you to lie down."

Finn stared at him. This was his big piece of wisdom?

"I know you want to help your brother, but you can't. You don't know what you're doing. So no matter what happens, who you see, what they ask of you, do nothing. Even if another Dreamwalker is the one doing the asking."

"I thought we were the good guys."

"Just because someone gets a gift doesn't mean they always know how to use it well. There will be things you cannot understand, and I can't teach you enough tonight to protect you. So I just want you to lie down and, if you can, go to sleep in your dream."

Finn wanted to throw up, and not just because the tea had tasted so wretched.

Dreamwalker.

It was a happy-sounding word, but as far as she could tell, not many happy things came from it.

FIVE

It was one thirty in the morning when Rafe pulled up in front of Finn's house. She'd been at the gym for almost four hours, and she was exhausted. She assumed the rotten-tasting tea had something to do with it.

"Want me to walk you to the door?"

"No. I'm fine."

"Yeah, you look fine." She glared at him, and he laughed. "Very fierce." And then whatever fun they were having was over. "Remember—"

"I know. Lie down and go to sleep. In the dream. You've said it twenty times."

"Because it's important. I'll pick you up in the morning at eight."

"I've got school."

"Call in sick."

"You know, I want to pass my classes so I can get into college and have a life."

"I'd like you to have a life, too. That's why I'm going to pick you up at eight." It hung there, the implication of what he was saying. He realized he'd gone too far because his tone changed immediately. "Have a friend get the homework for you. This will be like the flu. You'll be back before you know it."

Finn reached for the door handle but didn't pull it to get out. She turned back to him. "What happens if I don't just lie down and go to sleep?" ·

Rafe slowly unwrapped a piece of sugarless cinnamon gum.

"Maybe nothing. Maybe you wake up in the morning feeling great and have a delicious bowl of oatmeal for breakfast. Or ... maybe, whatever you're most afraid of grabs you and won't let go. It squeezes you until you can't breathe and convinces you everything you care about is going to be destroyed and there's not a damn thing you can do. Then that demon lets you go and laughs as you cry. And you keep crying, long after you wake up."

He put the gum in his mouth and chewed it. The scent of cinnamon filled the car.

"You're just trying to make sure I do what you say."

"Yep."

Finn climbed out of the car. It was really cold outside.

Her grandmother was asleep on the chair next to Noah's bed. Finn felt bad leaving her there, but she knew if Nana woke up she'd want to talk about Finn's session with Rafe, and the poor woman wouldn't be able to go to sleep afterward. Finn grabbed a blanket from the sofa and draped it over Nana before heading to bed.

Finn didn't know what to think anymore. Her grandmother clearly believed in whatever this was. But Finn didn't want to. What she wanted was for Noah to get better and her life to go back to the way it was before, as lame as that might have seemed to everyone else. She wanted to worry about math tests and learning how to parallel park. She didn't want to worry about whether she'd wake up crying and never be able to stop.

But what if something was keeping Noah in that coma? What if her brother could be saved and she was the only one who could do it? If there was even a little bit of truth in that, she had to try.

She pulled off her jeans and T-shirt and put on a ratty pair of sweatpants and a hoodie. In the dreams she'd had so far, she'd been wearing the clothes she'd gone to sleep in. Who knew where she was going tonight, and if she was going to have to lie down, she didn't want to worry about getting her favorite clothes dirty. Even subconsciously dirty.

She sat on the bed. Only then did she see Eddie sitting at her door, staring at her.

"You worried about me? Or just wondering why everyone's acting so weird?"

As if to answer, the dog walked over and jumped onto her bed. He waited until she lay down, and then he nestled next to her.

Finn closed her eyes.

It was quiet in the house.

Eddie's breath was warm against her hand. *What does he know that I don't?* Finn thought. She lay there, trying to see the world through Eddie's eyes. *Does he understand what people say? Does he dream? Does he worry about what happens when we die?* Finn wondered all these things until she finally fell asleep.

She felt a vibration through her feet. She looked up and saw a light moving out of a tunnel carved into a mountain.

A train. She was in the middle of a train track. She tried to step over a rail to safety, but it suddenly shot up and was as high as her waist. She went to climb over it again and then heard a dog barking.

She turned. Eddie stood on the wooden crossties of the track. At least, it looked like Eddie. A tiny, tiny Eddie. Like a toy. He barked again.

"Come here, boy."

He ignored her and lay down.

Finn looked up. The train was only a few hundred feet away. The whistle blew. In the engine car, someone was waving furiously and pulling on the whistle cord.

He looked familiar. Who was it?

Moby Dawson. What was Moby doing in her dream?

Tiny toy Eddie barked again. She looked at the dog and watched him stand up and then lie down again.

You've got to be kidding, *she thought.*

She got down flat, pressed her face against the crossties. She waited for the massive train to crush her. She closed her eyes and tried to block out the roar and rumble of the train until—

It stopped. All she could hear was the wind whistling. Finn opened her eyes.

She was falling. Around her, lightning lit up the sky. She screamed. Her voice sounded like thunder. Almost immediately, a flash of lightning snaked out from a cloud and slammed into the middle of her forehead, sending a shooting pain through her body.

She kept falling. The ground grew closer, and then she—

Fell through it to an even darker place. Where was Eddie? What was happening? She was supposed to go to sleep. But how was she supposed to do that? Her hair whipped across her face, stinging her eyes. Why hadn't Rafe told her this could happen? Why hadn't he told her what to do? She started to cry. She needed help. She couldn't do this on her own. She needed someone to——

She stopped falling.

There was a hand on Finn's shoulder, holding her. Six inches in front of her face, white sand. She heard waves crash onto a nearby shore.

The hand gently flipped her over and laid her on the beach. Towering above her, Finn saw a beautiful Asian woman, maybe the most beautiful person she'd ever seen in her entire life. The woman wore black silk pants and a purple top. Her hair cascaded from a ponytail on the top of her head. Even though it was dark, Finn could see her face clearly because the woman wore a thin, twisted cord around her neck. It was lit by a violet light that reminded Finn of flowers.

Finn felt underdressed in her sweatpants.

"I'm Wan," the woman said. Finn knew Wan wasn't speaking English, that she was talking in a language Finn had never heard before. Yet Finn understood what she was saying.

"You're a Dreamwalker," Finn said.

"As are you."

Wan pointed to Finn's neck. Finn reached up, touched a necklace. She saw its bright white light reflected on her hands.

"I'm not really a Dreamwalker," Finn replied. "I'm just supposed to lie down and go to sleep. So I don't hurt myself."

Wan nodded, then drew a silver sword from the scabbard slung across her back. The sword's hilt was encrusted with bright objects. They were moving. Finn looked closer and realized they were bugs— beetles, ladybugs, others she'd never seen before. They looked like precious gems.

Wan sat on the sand next to Finn and crossed her legs. She rested her sword on her lap.

"What are you doing?" Finn asked. She remembered Rafe's warning about rogue Dreamwalkers. Though nothing about this woman seemed the least bit dangerous.

"I am going to make sure you go to sleep. And that nothing keeps you from staying asleep."

"You're helping me?"

"Yes."

"Why?"

"Because you asked me to."

"I did?"

"Yes. From the very depths of your soul."

"Why you?"

"I simply got here first." She gestured, and Finn looked to where she pointed. A host of shadowy figures, men and women of what looked to be every race, creed, and color hovered above her. Their essence slowly faded as Finn watched. When they had all gone, Wan put her hand over Finn's eyes.

A feeling of safety washed over her, and Finn was asleep before she could say thank you.

SIX

Her phone was buzzing. She opened her eyes. It was light outside. Finn reached for her neck, to see if the Lochran was there. It wasn't. There was nothing to prove that what she dreamed was anything more than the random firing of electricity in her brain. But somehow she knew, just knew, that Wan had watched over her all night.

Something moved on the bed. Eddie was staring at her. "I'm in one piece," Finn told him. And with that, he hopped off the bed and headed down the hall to take his place by Noah's bed. Finn reached for the phone. The phone buzzed again.

She reached over and saw a text from Jed. *Frzing in front of my house. Where R U?*

Finn checked the time. She was way late. She picked up the phone and then remembered that Rafe was coming to get her. She wasn't going to school today.

She typed: *Sick. Sorry. HMWK plz.*

The phone buzzed again. *Puke?*

Jed loved the details of any infirmity. If only he would focus on his grades, he would be a great doctor.

No puke, she wrote. *Fever. Need . . .*

She was about to type "sleep," but sleep was the last thing she wanted. She backed up her cursor and watched the *d, e, e,* and *n* disappear. She pushed Send as she threw her feet over the side of the bed.

She smelled bacon. Nana was already up.

Finn pushed herself out of bed and headed to the kitchen. "Morning, Nana."

"Why didn't you wake me when you got in?"

"You deserved a good night's sleep."

Nana smiled. "I woke up at three when my head bobbed."

"Was I sleeping peacefully the forty times you checked on me?"

Nana smiled and started to pull bacon from the pan and put it on a piece of paper towel. "Breakfast will be ready soon."

"I'm running late."

"I called Rafe and told him you were still asleep. We're supposed to let him know when you're dressed." It took Nana a long time to ask the question that Finn knew was coming. "How did it go?"

"I still don't like him, but I did what you asked. I stayed. Then when I came home, I did what he told me."

"Which was what?"

"Nothing. I lay down in my dream, and a woman with a sword watched me all night."

Nana's eyebrows raised just a touch, but she didn't ask more questions. Instead she said, "I finally reached your mother. A storm blew up in the North Sea. She's trapped for a couple of days."

Finn knew there was more to the conversation than that, but before she could ask, Nana said, "And the nurse was here first thing. She agreed with us about Noah's breathing. She's going to have the doctor order him an antibiotic, just in case. Maybe you have medical school in your future."

"You obviously don't remember my grade in freshman biology."

Nana smiled. It was more sad than happy.

Finn wanted to hug her but was afraid it would seem like too big a deal if she did. "I'm going to go say good morning."

Finn held Noah's hand in hers. It always surprised her how soft his skin was. The nurses said they'd never had a comatose patient with healthier skin. No doubt it was the herb goo Nana rubbed on him every day.

All the times she'd sat at his bedside—talked to him, studied with him, taken care of him—she'd never thought about his being anywhere but in this bed.

But now . . . Finn knew he was someplace else.

He was lost in a world that was as big and crazy as her town was small and ordinary. Wherever he was, he was reaching out to her. And the effort might be killing him. If she didn't hurry, he might never come back.

Finn started to cry. She fought the urge to run out of the room to hide her tears.

She had no idea where he was or how to find him. She just knew that she had to. She pulled her brother's hand to her lips and kissed it.

"Hang in there, Noah," she whispered. "I'm coming to get you."

SEVEN

Rafe was waiting in the car when Finn stepped outside. A brisk breeze blew the exhaust in little swirls around his tailpipe.

Finn opened the door and climbed in. He looked at her.

"A beautiful woman caught me as I was plummeting through space and then put me to sleep, promising to use her giant bug-covered sword to keep anyone from bothering me."

Rafe burst out laughing.

"Are you laughing because that's funny or because it's ridiculous?"

"There's nothing ridiculous about dreams, Finn. Nothing at all."

He started the car.

It was only when they'd driven halfway across town that Finn realized he hadn't really answered her question.

There were several people working out in the gym when they arrived. Rafe gave a couple of them instructions as he walked by: how to turn their torso to add power to their punches, a suggestion for different footwork. It seemed like he knew what he was talking about, or at least had convinced these people he did.

They finally made their way to the bottom of the stairs.

"Honestly, what's with the stairs?"

Rafe didn't answer, just headed up. Finn followed, putting her feet where he'd put his. She almost bumped into him when he stopped midway.

"There are a million ways to come up these stairs safely. Every one of them requires focus. You can't storm up in anger, and only the rarest of people could run up without killing themselves."

"So it's a security system?"

"In a manner of speaking."

"Who do you need protection from?"

"I don't know, but there's a reason your friend from last night carried a bug-covered sword."

When they got into his room, Rafe peeled off his coat and hung it over a set of antlers that were nailed to the wall by the door. Finn didn't remember them from last night, and they seemed wildly out of place. He crossed to the table, where two ceramic mugs sat next to a leather-bound book. He gestured for Finn to take a seat next to him and handed her one of the mugs.

"Little early in the day for sleep-inducing tea, isn't it?"

"It's water. Important to stay hydrated."

Was he joking? She took a sip. It was water.

Rafe pushed the leather-bound book toward her. "That's your homework."

Finn recognized the engraving of an animal trapped in a tangle of vines on the spine. She'd seen the book in Noah's room. She flipped through a few pages. They were covered with old-fashioned script and drawings of fantastical creatures and maps.

"What does a dusty book have to do with anything?"

"It's the journal of Sydney Norwich, an eighteenth-century British mystic. It's the best explanation of Dreamwalking I've ever found. I think there are things in here that might help you."

"I've got enough homework for school."

Rafe shifted toward her just a little bit. Finn realized he'd done it a couple of times last night, too. She glanced at his right hand. It was clenched. The skin on the knuckles was tight. He was angry. Finn was about to take a step back when he took a breath. She watched his fingers uncurl.

"Noah read every book I gave him," Rafe spat out. "He did every exercise, drank every mug of crap I pushed his way. He was smart, agile, and intuitive. If you're going to have a rat's ass chance of helping him, you need to be better than he was. And so far, you're not."

"Okay, okay," Finn said, trying to pacify him.

It didn't work. He leaned close. She could feel his breath on her cheek. "When you're dreaming, your job is to lie down, until I say you can do something else. And when we're working, your job is to do what I ask. Got it?"

Finn shrugged, and apparently Rafe took the gesture for consent, because he stood up and moved to the center of the room.

Finn wanted to tell him to piss off, but she followed him instead.

He raised his hands into a boxing stance. "Arms up."

Finn stared at him. "Just so you know, I'm going to listen. I'd just like to know why we're doing what we're doing."

"The woman in your dream last night. Big sword?"

"Yep."

"You think she was carrying it because it matched her shoes and purse? No. It's because you never know what a dream will bring. You have to be ready. You must honor the logic of the dream and be prepared for anything . . . everything. You might have to box, wrestle, rock climb . . ."

"Rock climb?" she asked. "I can barely text and walk at the same time."

"Dreams aren't like this world, Finn. Nobody can fly in this reality, but everyone can fly in their dreams. If you can imagine something, you can do it in the dream space, even if you could never do it in life. I need to introduce you to things so you can use them when you need them. We are going to practice so you can feel more confident. And all of this is about mastering the one thing you must master in order to survive."

"'Survive' is a big word."

He kept waiting, hands up. Silent.

"What do I have to master to survive?"

"Fear."

He said it very matter-of-factly, as if mastering fear were easy. Finn knew it wasn't. She was in high school. Fear was homeroom.

She lifted her hands and mirrored his stance.

Rafe showed Finn how to punch and then how to shift her weight to deliver the maximum force. He brought out a punching bag and made her hit it over and over and over again, holding his hand on her stomach until he was sure that she was using her core. Afterward, they moved to karate kicks. Snap kicks. Roundhouses. She used leverage to throw Rafe over her body. With every different thing they learned, he'd tell her to concentrate on her breathing: to make punches stronger, to slow down her heart, and to calm her mind; connecting to herself through breathing was the only reality she could absolutely control.

"If you can force yourself to breathe in critical moments," Rafe said, "you might survive whatever . . ." He left the thought hanging there.

His "might" did not inspire confidence. When she bent over to put her hands on her knees to rest, she realized she couldn't feel her arms. She didn't think Rafe would care, but she told him anyway. To her surprise, he laughed and said she could sit down. He headed to the kitchen and got her another mug of something, then sat on the floor next to her.

"I want you to drink it and then close your eyes. Start breathing. Make your exhales longer than the inhales, count if you need to. Then, when you're ready, move into the dream space."

"All those movies I saw?"

"Yes, the River of Dreams. Every dream being dreamed right now. Billions of people, asleep, wrestling with their subconscious in some way. I always found it quite beautiful, though I understand it can be overwhelming. You need to get comfortable so you can enter the River confidently. Fear is—"

"Bad. You've made that very clear."

"Then I will count today as a success."

Finn smiled despite herself and immediately regretted it.

"You have the power to go into any dream you choose," he told her. "So close your eyes, go into the River, grab a dream, and . . . try to fly."

"Fly?"

"Not too high."

Finn picked up the mug and got a whiff of something disgusting. "You need to stop drugging me."

"They're not drugs. They're herbs. Big difference."

She and Rafe sat in silence. "I know this is hard," he finally said. "If you're not ready, I understand. I'm sure Noah understands, too."

Finn knew he brought up Noah to manipulate her, and it worked. Finn drank the brown sludge. It coated her throat all the way down. She tossed the mug in Rafe's direction and closed her eyes before he caught it.

She made a silent wish for a few drops of sludge to fly out and stain his shirt.

Finn took a deep breath. Then another. She pushed Rafe out of her mind, as well as the aches in her arms and legs. She inhaled: one, two, three, four, five, six, seven. She exhaled: one, two, three, four, five, six, seven, eight.

She took another breath.

Inhale: one, two, three, four, five, six, seven.

Exhale: one, two, three, four, five, six, seven, eight.

Her body felt full, as if she were being inflated like a balloon. The parts of her she thought were real began to push away from one another.

And then she saw it!

Instead of darkness, color and movement, like a sheet of opaque plastic hung in front of an open window. She walked through the shimmering wall . . .

And into the River of Dreams.

She'd seen it through that tiny hole the night she saw her father. But this was different. Through the hole, it was like watching a chaotic movie. This . . . this was like watching a million movies while standing in a wind tunnel. The images flowed by her, over her, below her. Her ears were full of a humming, all the sounds in the dreams merging together.

There was nothing else to see. Nothing else to hear.

Nothing, except the feelings.

Joy, anger, love, fear, confusion. All bombarding Finn from the dreams that sped by. She could hardly keep up, and suddenly understood what Rafe meant by the River swallowing you. There was so much of it.

Too much.

She wanted to do what he'd told her to do and get out.

Get home.

Finn grabbed at an image as it flowed by. It pushed away everything around it, leaving only a single vision: two whales, one small, one large. The small whale was swallowing the larger one. Its body stretched and pulled as the larger whale struggled to escape. Finn saw fear in the eyes of the larger whale. She wanted to comfort it, but before she could do anything, the image disappeared.

Finn found herself back in the River.

Only now, it smelled like something had died. She heard something roar and turned toward the sound.

Something was running straight at her. A nightmare. A man with the head of a buffalo, covered in flaming sores and holding a glowing stick. He grabbed at her neck before she could get out of its way. One of the flaming sores burned her cheek.

Without thinking, she punched the creature in the face, hitting it just as Rafe showed her. It stumbled back a step, then lunged for her again. She jumped and was suddenly twenty feet in the air. Flying. The creature lumbered beneath her and roared in anger before being caught in the River and swept away.

Her heart pounded.

The creature was gone. She was safe, but what now? She

looked around. Something shimmered above her, the same opaque curtain.

She swam toward it, pushed through, and then—

Opened her eyes.

Finn felt queasy.

She saw Rafe's lips moving, knew he was talking to her, but she couldn't hear what he said. His face was out of focus. She blinked, hoping that would help. But he melted away and then . . .

Everything went black.

Rafe was sitting beside her when she woke up. He'd put a pillow under her head and covered her with a blanket. Finn tried to tell him. About being attacked. How she'd punched the way he'd taught her.

"What was it?" she asked him.

"I don't know." He rubbed his hands through his hair.

Talking had given her a headache. She watched Rafe chew on a nail. He was scared. All those days in the hospital with her mother and Nana, she recognized that look in people's eyes.

"Why did it attack me?" she asked.

It took him a long time to finally answer. "I've never heard of a Dreamwalker doing what you just did," he said. "Accessing the dream world when they're awake. When you told me what happened at school the other day, I just wondered if it was possible. And now I'm wondering if . . . what you saw, what attacked you . . . if it's somehow related. If you can access something that other Dreamwalkers can't, who knows what sorts of things might find their way to you."

"I don't know what I'm doing. I don't need horrible, burning creatures, too."

He just shook his head. Not agreeing with her, but mystified by all of it. After a moment, he told her he had a kickboxing lesson downstairs.

She was certain he was lying, that he'd screwed up somehow and needed to figure out what to do. She didn't care. She wanted to get away from him, too.

Finn asked if she could go home, but Rafe said no. They had things to talk about. He suggested she meditate while he was gone.

Finn had no idea how to meditate, so she just lay on the floor and stared at the ceiling. She wanted to go outside and clear her head. Do something crazy like drink a Red Bull and eat a Pop-Tart. She was also tempted to poke around the room and see what she could learn about Rafe, but one of the things that she'd already learned is that he moved without making a sound. She was certain he would be right next to her before she realized he was back. He wouldn't be excited to find her spying on him.

When she stood up, she saw Sydney Norwich's book on the table.

She crossed over and picked it up. There was a shiny spot

on the cover where, for hundreds of years, people had grabbed the book to open it. When she flipped to the yellowed and water-stained title page, it read:

THE NARRATIVE OF MY LIFE

A Story of Time Spent in Between This World and Others,
with Hopes That It Will Guide Some and Give Peace to Others

By Sydney Norwich, Somersetshire

Finn had to squint to read the subtitle: "A Story of Time Spent in Between This World and Others, with Hopes That It Will Guide Some and Give Peace to Others."

She turned to the first page and started reading.

I was born in Somersetshire in the year of our Lord Seventeen Hundred and Twelve. My father was a sailor. He left home when I was three, never to be seen again. Whether he stayed away of his own accord or was swallowed by the ocean deep, my mother and I never knew, and there was no time to find out. Our lives were hard.

In my sixteenth year I began to have visions. At first, I thought they were reflective of an illness of the mind, but it became clear these visions were something else, something real. I could go to places other people could only imagine. And whilst in those places I could help other poor souls with the problems that afflicted them. As it became known I had this skill, people rewarded me for using it on their behalf, and I was able to secure a comfortable life for my beloved mother.

I am happy to say that I was able to provide for her until her death and that she never knew the pain these visions caused me.

For those who continue to read of my adventures, know that they are true as much as I know the truth and that I always sought to do right as well as I could.

Finn tore through the first twenty pages, which told how one night, after months of fitful sleep, Sydney dreamed a vivid dream about Charlotte, a beautiful girl from a nearby village. In the dream, a wall of fire was chasing her. Sydney sprouted wings, picked her up, and flew her to a giant nest on a mountaintop. She kept asking him for help, but despite his repeated questions about what kind of help she needed, she couldn't or wouldn't say.

The next day, unable to get the dream out of his head, Sydney walked several miles to Charlotte's house and discovered her entire family sick with fever. Charlotte was near death. Sydney fetched a local healer, and Charlotte was saved.

From that moment on, his nights were filled with other people's dreams and nightmares. Sydney, mild-mannered in life, became like one of King Arthur's knights in his dreams: saving women, slaying dragons, taking animal form to rescue children, or simply standing and protecting those who did not have the will to run away from whatever danger threatened them.

Even though a part of him feared the experiences weren't real, Sydney felt a responsibility to help all these people in his dreams and was deeply sad when he couldn't. It was a difficult burden to carry alone, and he finally revealed to his mother what was happening. Afraid her son might be possessed, she pleaded with him to stop helping people and to keep the visions to himself.

Sydney obeyed her until he dreamed about the local vicar.

In the dream, the man was an earthworm forced to burrow to the center of the earth. The earthworm wanted to see sunlight but knew he never would. He begged Sydney to fill the hole above him with dirt and end his torment. Instead, Sydney leaped into the hole and gave the earthworm comfort. Up close, he saw it was covered in chalky dust. When Sydney awoke, he knew the vicar was in danger somewhere along the local chalky cliffs. And, the next morning, he set out to find him.

After a full day's search, he found the vicar at the bottom of a twenty-foot embankment. He'd tripped while out for a walk and fallen down the cliffside. He'd broken his ankle, so he couldn't save himself. Without Sydney's help, the vicar would have died from exposure.

The vicar asked Sydney how he found him. According to the memoir, Sydney considered lying but decided lying to a man of God was a poor choice, so he told the vicar the truth: The vicar had come to him in a dream and asked for help. Sydney had used the clues from the dream to find him. *"The merciful Lord,"* the vicar exclaimed in church the following Sunday, *"has touched Sydney with his hand and given me a miracle."* With this blessing, Sydney came out of hiding and put his gift to work.

Sydney's story was riveting, but Finn was tired. She flipped ahead to see how long the book was. And there, near the end, she saw a drawing.

A triangle inside a circle inside a square.

All of it inside a maze.

And next to the maze, a black bird. The illustration was titled "The Labyrinth and the Black Grouse."

It was too similar to what she'd seen in Noah's journal to be a coincidence.

Sydney Norwich had been to the last place Noah had written about. This is why Rafe had given it to her: Long-dead Sydney Norwich might be the key to finding and saving her brother.

She had to get home. Finn closed Sydney's memoir, grabbed her coat, and headed for the door.

EIGHT

Finn snuck out of the gym while Rafe had his back to the door. She read more of Sydney's book on the bus.

The chapter with the maze involved Sydney's attempt to help a pregnant woman named Molly. Her dreams were more tortured than any Sydney had experienced. Many of them involved her husband, Peter. Molly told Sydney that since she'd gotten pregnant, Peter had changed. He left home for long periods. He'd started carrying a knife. He'd come home more than once with bruised knuckles, like he'd been hitting his hand against something hard. The blood on his cuffs made her think it was another person.

Sydney had been a Dreamwalker for almost forty years. He had helped thousands of people with problems big and small. But this situation "bedeviled" him.

Molly believed Peter was in the grip of Satan himself. Before I knew the truth, I foolishly assured her

Satan had no time for the dreams of men. There was too much for him to do in the waking world. But later, I came to believe I was wrong. For a great evil was afoot, and whatever good had once been in Peter's soul had long since been trampled by it.

Sydney worked for weeks to figure out what was afflicting Peter. Each night, he followed Peter in his dreams and eventually had an experience he had never had before.

Peter didn't have the same kind of glowing necklace Sydney did, at least not one that he could see, but Sydney realized that Peter still moved through the River of Dreams just how a Dreamwalker would. Sydney wondered if he was a more powerful being, or if some other magic allowed him to move through the dream space. Whatever it was, Peter was active and focused, returning to the same people's dreams over and over to torment them, creating nightmares. How could he do this? Sydney wondered. And why? What drove him to this evil?

As Sydney followed Peter, he went into levels of the dream world that Sydney had never seen before, dark places full of fear, dripping with evil. In one of these places, Sydney saw Peter bow to something in the shadows. Sydney couldn't get a good look at who or what it was. But Peter's deference made it clear that this being was important. So when Peter headed off, Sydney stayed, waiting for it to emerge. It never did.

Eventually, though, a black grouse—Sydney's favorite bird—flew out of the shadows and landed at Sydney's feet. Its musical trill was the only beauty in this dark place. The bird hopped back to the shadows, asking Sydney to follow it. Sydney's curiosity pulled him forward.

The bird led him through a cold and horrifying tunnel. When Sydney emerged from it, he found a large pool of water. Black, still as death. The grouse stood at the water's edge. When Sydney approached, the bird stepped into the pool. Sydney followed the bird until they were both in over their heads. He had no trouble breathing underwater, and, deep in the pool, Sydney saw a gold door. Opening it, he found himself inside a maze. He started to explore, being careful to mark a path so he could find his way out.

He followed the bird over several evenings, trying to work his way through the maze. Each night, he failed and was forced to turn around and leave the way he'd entered. Finally, one night he was so engrossed in the search he forgot to exercise the caution that had allowed him to make his way out of the maze. He got lost.

As he frantically looked for a way home, he encountered something so terrifying he felt it burn his soul like the fires of hell and fill his mind with madness.

Sydney tried to fight his way out but was exhausted from his time in this underworld. He could not save himself, and, his soul scorching with a kind of pain he didn't think possible, he felt compelled to reach for the twisted cord around his neck. He ripped at it, and the Lochran tore. He was expelled from the dream world.

Forever.

Sydney never dreamed another dream. His sleep was undisturbed. Empty of visions, both good and evil. My sleep is a blank slate. I am left waiting for the day when God's own hand might deign to write something upon it.

Much to Finn's frustration, Sydney Norwich stubbornly refused to reveal what sort of evil he had faced, what the "it" was that had "filled his mind with madness." All he would say was that when he woke from that final dream, he was bedridden for a month.

What would have happened if Sydney hadn't broken the Lochran? Finn wondered. If he hadn't found his way out of the maze, would he have lapsed into a coma, too? And, if the maze was related to why Noah was in a coma, what had drawn him to it? Was he following someone like Molly's husband, someone intent on doing evil in the dream world? And, if Noah was dealing with something terrifying, why hadn't he talked to Rafe or Nana?

When she finally got home, Finn's hands and face were tingling from the cold. She burst through the front door, glad for the blast of heat that hit her as she did.

It was only when she was walking past the couch in the living room that she saw Moby Dawson. He was sitting with her grandmother, holding a mug of hot chocolate. If he was here, school must be over. Finn had no idea so much time had gone by. "Hi, Moby," Finn said, startled.

"Uh, hi, Finn. I heard you were sick."

Nana jumped in. "I told him you were feeling much better and had taken a walk to stretch your legs."

Finn rubbed her freezing hands together. "It was colder than I expected."

Moby reached for a stack of papers on the table. "There was a reading assignment for New World History. It's long. I thought you might want to get a head start." He handed it to her.

"Thanks."

"No problem."

This was now the longest conversation they'd had since he'd moved to town. He'd been in her dream last night. Now he was in her living room.

Her grandmother stood up. "Fionnuala, Seth and I were enjoying some hot chocolate. How about I get you some?"

Finn watched Nana walk to the kitchen.

"Seth?"

"My real name. Fionnuala . . . I assume you don't want me using that at school?"

She smiled. "If you don't mind . . . Seth."

"I've gotten used to Moby."

They stared at each other. *Why was he in my dream?* Before she'd thought of a good reason, she blurted out, "That couch is older than Nana. Why don't we hang in my room?"

The boy formerly known as Moby picked up his mug and followed Finn down the hall.

Seth scanned the books on her shelf.

"You read."

"So do you."

"I mean you like to read. And do it when no one's grading you."

"People usually leave you alone if you're reading." Which was true; Finn just had no idea why she'd said it. Making conversation. "How was school today?" she asked, making some more.

"Fine."

He picked up a book from the shelf. It was a book of poetry her father had given her in sixth grade. Poems about nature.

"I haven't read any of those in a long time," she told him.

Moby flipped to a page in the book marked by a folded-down corner. He started reading and then stopped almost as quickly. "I should go," he said, putting the book back on the shelf. He barely made eye contact as he rushed from the room.

How weird.

Why did he bother to bring her the homework?

She thought back to last night's dream, remembered the look of panic on his face as he stood in the cab of the train engine.

She suddenly realized he wasn't in her dream; she'd dropped into *his*, one where he was out of control, traveling too fast. He'd needed help, and Finn, as a Dreamwalker, had responded, even if she hadn't meant to. *I got pulled there to help*, she thought. *But I made it so much worse. He dreamed he crushed me with a train.* He came to make sure she was okay, even though he probably had no idea why he felt he needed to. They were connected, if only by the subconscious experience of fear. Messing with other people's dreams was not something to be taken lightly.

Finn crossed to the bookshelf and pulled out the book. She opened it to the page he'd been looking at, a poem titled "Vapors." One of the passages was underlined. It read,

> And if you see it,
> Run.
> Not fast, not slow,
> But at a speed that keeps.
> Run.
> For the mists are chasing you.

Finn had no memory of the poem or the passage. Her father must have highlighted it, though she couldn't imagine why. It was super depressing.

When Finn heard the phone ring, she knew it was Rafe, wondering where the hell she was. She headed toward the kitchen. Nana was hanging up the phone. Before she could say anything, Finn volunteered, "He'd beat up on me enough for one day."

"Fair enough." Nana slid a dish into the oven, fish and some sort of vegetable. "He said to do the same as last night. I'll make the tea for you."

Finn sat down.

"And your mom called while you were over there. She wanted to check on you."

"She doesn't need to worry about me."

"I hope you take this in the spirit I intend . . . You're dumber than I thought if you think she can stop worrying about you."

"I will take that in the spirit you intend."

Nana smiled. "The storm's supposed to clear tomorrow. Hopefully, she'll be here the day after." Nana closed the oven door. She stood quietly for a moment, looking at Finn, then said, "I'm going to ask how it went, but just know that your brother always said 'good.'"

Finn gave her grandmother the highlights, leaving out how much her body hurt, how—because she'd fainted and he didn't have any idea why—she still didn't have any faith in Rafe. She also left out the part about the drawing in Sydney Norwich's book matching Noah's journal and how she was afraid that Noah was getting sicker because he was trying to reach out to Finn.

From the way her grandmother squeezed her hand as they talked, Finn could tell that Nana was scared. There didn't seem to be any reason to add to it.

Finn pulled Noah's journal from underneath his bed and tucked it into her sweatshirt. She didn't want Nana to see it and decide to put it back wherever it had been hidden until yesterday.

She leaned over and gave him a kiss on the forehead.

"If you moved through people's dreams the way you moved through video games, you must have been amazing."

Finn watched her brother, waited, hoped for some sign he was in there and trying to get home. But all he did was breathe, a little more labored than earlier that day. In, out. In, out.

In, out.

In.

Out.

In.

Out.

NINE

Finn checked her phone when she got back to her room. There was a message from Jed.

Puke yet?

No. Feeling better, she wrote back.

Okay, good.

A few minutes later, she got a string of emojis: a piece of pie, a crescent moon, and a smiley face with both eyes closed. This was a game they played: random emojis intended to communicate a simple thought. A pie and a crescent moon were both parts of something, she thought. Maybe he was simply saying we are all connected? She quickly dismissed it as too philosophical for Jed. Pie is food. Dessert. Her favorite. Whenever they had pie at the cafeteria, Jed would make fun of her because she always said, "Pie is good."

Pie, crescent moon, smiley face with both eyes closed. Good. Night. Sleep.

He was wishing her a good night's sleep.

Jed didn't know that wasn't possible. She wished she'd told him about the dreams. Maybe she would. Tomorrow. Maybe he could help her make sense of everything. For now, she just typed *U get good nights sleep 2* and hit Send.

Finn didn't want her grandmother to see her working with Noah's dream journal, so she did homework until Nana delivered the mug of tea.

That had been a half hour ago, and the tea was still sitting on Finn's night table. She picked it up and stared at it. She wanted to be clearheaded so she could stay up and read Noah's journal. She needed to figure out how to follow him, how to find him.

Finn picked up the mug and tiptoed out of her room. She listened for her grandmother. The house was quiet. Finn continued to the bathroom and poured the tea into the toilet and flushed it away. Only then did her heart start pounding.

Had she just made a terrible mistake?

Finn climbed into bed. She pushed aside the feeling she was intruding into her brother's private thoughts and opened the notebook. His hurt feelings were something they could talk about when he woke up.

Noah started the journal after having strange and vivid dreams about a boy named Jason, who he knew only from summer camp. For over a week, Noah lived through horrifying dreams that Jason was being attacked from within.

Jason's insides would fall out of him: heart, intestines, lungs. As Finn deciphered his notes, she sensed Noah's struggle to figure out what the images meant and what he could do to help Jason. He'd gone to dream-analysis websites and looked up symbols. He held Jason's organs in the dreams, hoping he could put them back inside his body. Eventually, when Noah realized he couldn't stop what was happening, he just sat with Jason in the dreams while the young man writhed in pain. Noah eventually called Jason in real life, hoping a conversation would end the dreams altogether.

Finn wondered how that conversation had gone. "Hey, I've been having these strange dreams about you" seemed like an awkward starting place, but he'd obviously stumbled on some magic formula because the words *Mom. Sick.* were scribbled next to Jason's phone number. Jason was "spilling his guts." The dreams showed that he needed someone to talk to.

At the very bottom of that page he'd written the word *Center* and a phone number. Finn picked up her phone and dialed it.

"This is the Center. How can I help you?" a woman asked.

"Uh, sorry," Finn mumbled. "I'm not sure this is the right number. What do you do there?"

"Counseling and support groups, sweetheart. For people dealing with illness and loss."

"Oh."

"You sure I can't help you in some way?"

The woman's voice was like honey. If she got you talking, there was no telling what you would say.

"No."

"You can always call back. We're here twenty—"

Finn cut her off. "Okay, thanks. Bye." She hung up, a lump in her throat. Noah found a way for Jason to talk. Finn flipped through the notebook. There were no more mentions of Jason. Maybe the nightmares had stopped. For both of them.

Finn kept reading.

Not long after that, Noah must have told Mom or Nana about the dreams, because Rafe's name started appearing. Noah continued to make detailed notes of what he experienced in the River, but they began to be interspersed with research in different-colored inks and theories about what various dreams meant and who the people he'd encountered in the dream space were and the kind of help they needed.

He wrote *Ask Rafe* about things big and small.

If a guy died in the dream, what happened to him in real life?

Did animals dream? How would you know? Were you supposed to help?

Could you refuse to help someone?

And what happened if you tried to help someone and failed?

As she got toward the end of the notebook, a new thread emerged, an ongoing experience that didn't seem attached to anyone. Noah was on a quest, tracking something through many levels. The fierce red-green-and-yellow hummingbird eventually appeared and led Noah to darker and more dangerous places. Finn saw a word reappear several times, the final time Noah had underlined it three times for emphasis. The word was *Malum*.

She crossed to her computer and typed it into an online dictionary.

Malum was Latin for "evil."

Even without the tea, Finn felt sleep stalking her. She feared what it might bring, but she knew she couldn't keep it at bay.

The last few nights had been hard on her, and now her body ached from the day with Rafe. Her eyes kept closing involuntarily. She looked at the empty mug on her nightstand, a part of her wondered if she should have taken it. *I'll just have to face what comes.*

With that brave thought, she fell asleep.

She stood in the River of Dreams.

Without Nana's or Rafe's herbs, the experience was totally different, a thousand times more powerful.

Rather than just a rush of images and sounds and feelings, Finn could pinpoint all of them. She could isolate anything she wanted: the image of a woman plunging into a flaming star, the sound of a baby laughing, the fear of a man fighting a three-headed dragon.

It was . . . overwhelming and amazing.

Rafe had been insistent that she do nothing until she was fully trained, that she should just lie down and sleep. But Noah was fading. He might be dying. If he came into the River looking for something, she needed to figure out what it was and where he went to find it. She couldn't wait until she was ready. She might never be ready.

Where to begin? What exactly should she look for in this vast flow of experiences?

Finn concentrated on Noah himself, on the maze, the symbols he'd drawn. She scanned for the hummingbird, the curls of smoke their father had blown Noah into. None of it worked. The man with the buffalo head was the only other idea she had, but it didn't seem like a good idea. He'd attacked her.

Finn was overwhelmed.

The River was too big. Maybe Rafe was right. She didn't know enough to find Noah. What if she was actually making things worse for him? She felt her stomach tense, a faint buzzing played at the edges of her awareness. And then she remembered what Rafe had said: Fear was the enemy.

So she couldn't give in to it. She had to . . . breathe.

Inhale. One, two, three, four.

Exhale. One, two three, four, five—

And then, she sensed her mother. Finn reacted and was pulled—

Someplace she'd never been. A beamed ceiling towered over a room full of dark furniture, heavy, solid pieces that looked as if they had been made by hand a long time ago. The walls were bright white, as if to offset the bleak landscape through the window. Across the room, her mother was frantically searching through a chest of drawers.

Finn was in her mother's dream.

She didn't want to be here. Let her mother figure out her own problems.

Finn knew that was kind of bitchy, but things were complicated. Her mother . . . she left. Finn understood the economics. They needed

*good health insurance. But Noah was in a coma. Who leaves a crisis
and heads to the other side of the earth? Finn didn't. Nana didn't.*

Parents aren't supposed to leave.

*Finn watched her mother open one drawer, then another, pull-
ing things out and throwing them to the floor. Finn couldn't stand it
anymore.* "Mom," *she finally said,* "What are you looking for?"

Her mother turned around. She looked so sad.

*Finn had never seen her like that before, even after her father died
in the crash. Through it all—the Coast Guard search, the horrible news,
the funeral—her mom had acted as if everything was the same: made
dinner, washed their clothes, kept their routines, made cakes and cookies.
When Finn woke up in the middle of the night and wanted to go to her
dad's grave, her mom took her, standing nearby as Finn cried . . .*

Like she didn't care.

*And now, here she was, bereft. Over what? Some missing neck-
lace or scarf?*

"Mom," *Finn repeated quietly.* "What are you looking for?"

Julia turned at the sound of Finn's voice, almost startled by it.
"You," *her mother gasped as tears ran down her face. Her mother
opened her arms. Finn didn't move. Her mother just stood there, arms
open. The choice had to be Finn's. But what was the right choice?
This was a dream, not their living room. Would it even matter?*

*She stood there, trying to decide what to do, until her mother
finally said,* "Finn," *in a voice that was too heartbroken to ignore.*

Finn walked into the embrace. "I'm right here," *she repeated.
Finn could hear the beating of her mother's heart. Was it only a
dream, or was this the beating of her real heart, so many miles away?*

Finn led her mother to the couch and sat her down.

"Why don't you go back to sleep," Finn suggested.

"I can't. I have to watch you."

"You'll see me soon."

Finn thought back to the Dreamwalker, Wan, who had helped her go to sleep. She helped her mother lie down and put a hand over her eyes. She watched her mother's body relax and the anxiety leave her face. After a minute, she was asleep.

Finn realized she was tired. So tired. Maybe she should do what Rafe said and just lie down, go to sleep in the dream, before she got hurt. She would look for Noah tomorrow.

Yes, that's what she'd do. Start again tomorrow. But then she heard a voice, a faint, "Help." She closed her eyes and heard it again, louder. "Help!"

A child. A girl. Finn knew she should go home, but somewhere, there was a child who needed help.

She concentrated on the voice and—

Was back in the River.

The young girl's voice broke through the roar. "Get away!" she screamed. "Leave me alone."

Finn reached out and was pulled into—

A forest.

The only light came from a sliver of moon in a starless sky and the glow of Finn's Lochran. The only sound was the crunch of dry leaves.

Someone was running off to Finn's left. She ran after them.

She swerved to avoid the limbs dangling near the ground. Then, out of nowhere, one caught her on the shoulder and knocked her down. She scrambled to her feet, trying to get her bearing as her eyes adjusted to the darkness. This was unlike any forest she'd ever seen. There was a reason she kept bumping into tree limbs. It wasn't just that the lower limbs of the trees were heavy and hanging near the ground.

The trees were alive.

A branch swung toward her head. Finn ducked, and it missed her.

She heard the girl shout, "Put me down!" It was coming from above her.

Another limb swung at Finn. When it got close, she jumped, higher than she'd ever jumped, higher than she had ever seen anyone jump. Finn landed on the limb and ran toward the trunk of the tree. The tree swayed back and forth, trying to shake her off. She struggled for balance but finally reached the trunk. She started climbing.

The tree growled in frustration, trying to throw Finn off, but she held on and kept moving. As the trunk narrowed, the motion became more violent. She needed to find the girl and get the hell out of here.

"Where are you?" Finn screamed, wind whistling past her ears.

There was no response. Finn stopped and clung to the trunk of the tree as it whipped back and forth. She closed her eyes and listened. She heard the sound of a muffled voice. The child was very near.

What now?

Finn remembered what Rafe had said: Honor the logic of the dream. Finn tried to stay calm. The logic of the dream: forest, trees, wood . . .

She held out her hand. On her palm, a flame sparked. She willed it to grow.

"Stop moving," she told the tree. "Or I will burn you down."

The swaying stopped.

Finn took a few tentative steps away from the trunk, steadying herself by holding on to the limb above her.

"Where is she?" When the tree didn't respond, she brought the fire closer to the needles on the branch next to her. They began to smoke, and the tree shuddered. Finn pulled the fire away. "Show me where she is," she insisted.

After a moment, a few trees over, a limb unfurled, revealing a young girl, probably no more than eight. She was wearing yellow-and-pink pajamas.

Finn held up the flame. "I'm going to throw this to you. Catch it. It won't hurt you. Hold the fire and tell the tree to put you down. Okay?"

The girl nodded. Finn could feel fear radiating from the child. Something was wrong in her life. Something was terribly wrong.

"Are you in second grade?"

"Third," the girl responded quietly.

"Do you like your teacher?" she asked, gently.

"Yes. Mrs. Bassett. She's nice."

"Run to Mrs. Bassett. Even when you wake up, go to her. Ask her for help." Finn saw fear in the child's eyes.

"I can't," she whispered.

"Yes, you can, sweetheart. The light will help you find your way. Mrs. Bassett will help you find your way."

She tossed the ball of fire toward the girl. Impossibly, it stayed lit as it flew through the air. The girl caught it. It lit up her face. She was beautiful.

"What about you?" the girl asked.

Finn smiled. "I'm going to be fine." Finn showed her hand, where another blue flame already sat on her palm.

"Put me down," the girl said to the tree, holding out her flame.

For a moment, nothing happened. The girl pressed the flame closer to the tree. It began to move, bowing like a servant before a king. Finn watched as the tree set the girl down on the forest floor. She followed the flame as it moved through the trees and into the distance. Finn realized she didn't know the girl's name. She'd ask Rafe if there was a way to find her and make sure she was safe.

Standing on top of the tree, Finn felt . . . powerful. She didn't know if she'd ever felt this way. At least, not in a long time.

She blew out her blue flame and was swallowed by the darkness. She was about to return to the River when, in the distance, she saw a circle of light. It grew brighter until she could see what was in the center of it: Noah, sitting in a tree, trying to get her attention.

"Noah! I'm coming."

She jumped across the span between her and the next tree. The limb flexed, and she used the movement to propel herself forward.

The circle dimmed.

"Hold on!" But even as she screamed the words, Noah's light

went out. Finn leaped to the place where he'd been. He was gone, but . . . there was something.

A hole in the air.

Blacker than night. Without thinking, Finn reached into it.

Her arm disappeared into cold nothingness. And exploded with pain.

She screamed and tried to pull her arm out of the void. Something was holding her, pulling at her. It was hard to breathe. Her head was full of a terrible buzzing. She anchored her foot against the tree and pushed with all her might, yanking against whatever was holding her until she finally fell backward, landing on the branch. Finn's arm was heavy. An eel, damp, glistening in the dim light of the crescent moon, had swallowed her arm up to the elbow. Without thinking, Finn slammed the eel on the branch. She lost her balance; she and the eel began to fall, bouncing from one limb to the next. She tried to get a handhold but couldn't. She finally landed, hard, on the forest floor.

The impact caused the eel to release its grip. She pulled her arm out of its mouth. It lay still, only its mouth moving, almost like it was talking.

Finn edged closer. A whisper, "Malum."

And then . . . the eel was gone, and Finn was filled with a terrible fear. "Noah!" she screamed. Her voice rang into the distance, then there was only silence, except for the roar of the blood in her body.

She was scared.

Keep breathing, she told herself.

Close your eyes and go to sleep.

Be strong for Noah.

Take one more breath.

Everything will be okay.

Everything will be ...

TEN

When Finn's alarm clock went off, she rolled over to hit the button and felt a piercing pain across her shoulders. She fell back onto her bed. It all flooded back: the fall out of the tree; the eel; the sense of Noah's absence, that he'd been swallowed, taken by something otherworldly.

But how her body felt didn't make sense. Dreams weren't real. She shouldn't hurt. Finn pushed herself up to a seated position and hit the alarm button to stop its blaring. She saw Eddie sitting in the door. Had he walked down to find out why it was taking so long to turn off the alarm?

"When I watched you run while you slept," Finn said to him, "I never thought you were actually going somewhere." He cocked his head sideways, looking at her curiously, and then turned to pad back to Noah's room.

Finn was glad she'd put a hat on because, at the speed she was walking, it was going to take all day to get to school, and it was cold outside. Nana was worried when she'd seen how slow Finn was moving, but Finn blamed it on Rafe. Finn felt bad for lying, but she needed to think things through.

She had so many questions and no confidence she could get answers by herself. She needed to talk to someone.

Jed was her only option.

Nana had offered to give Finn and Jed a ride to school, but Finn lied again, said she wanted the fresh air. What she really thought was that Jed would ask a lot of questions, and when he got interested in something, he talked louder. She didn't need the whole school wondering what a Dreamwalker was.

She'd texted Jed that she was leaving the house and to watch for her. She didn't want to have to take off her gloves to text him as she got close.

He was waiting at the sidewalk when she got there. He was not wearing a hat.

"You're going to freeze to death," she told him.

"I dried my hair," he replied, referring to his habit of coming outside right after his shower, regardless of the temperature. "Why are you walking like a ninety-year-old?"

"Long story."

"Apparently it's going to be a long, slow walk, so go ahead."

It was the opening she needed. Except, even though she'd thought about telling him what was going on, she hadn't actually thought about how she was going to say it.

She looked away. "God, it's cold out here."

"Are you pregnant?"

Finn laughed. "I haven't had a boyfriend since—"

She looked at Jed. His face was a mask of confusion and . . . something she couldn't quite read. The question was real.

"No, I'm not pregnant."

"Then why have you been acting so weird?"

So she told him.

Starting with the dreams, and then learning that Noah was a Dreamwalker and that she was a Dreamwalker. She told him about the lessons with Rafe, and how Rafe thought Noah was reaching out to her. She even told him about saving the little girl the night before, and the eel and Noah and Malum. When she finished, they were a block from school. Jed stopped and turned to face her. It had gotten really cold over the last fifteen minutes.

"Are you bullshitting me?" he asked matter-of-factly.

"No."

"If I call Nana, she'd say the same thing?"

"I haven't told her everything that's happened, but mostly."

He stood there, staring at her. It felt like forever. Then an impossibly large smile spread across his face.

"That's cool. Are you sure you're not crazy?"

"No."

She pulled Noah's journal from her backpack. She'd brought it so she could read it in the spare or boring moments that presented themselves. She flipped through it. "This is Noah's journal. He wrote down what he'd learned, the dreams he had. Some of the people he helped."

He stared intently as the pages went by. "The little guy was more artistic than I gave him credit for. But this isn't proof it happened. It's just proof he kept a journal."

"I told you I was in Moby's dream?"

"Yeah."

"He came to my house last night."

"Why?"

"He said to bring me homework. But I think we had some sort of dream . . . connection."

"Or he might like you."

"Until he came to my house, we'd barely spoken to each other."

"Who knows what he does with that computer of his. Maybe he came by to install a spy camera in your bedroom."

Finn was starting to think she was wrong to tell Jed, that there was no way anyone could accept that this was real. He'd stopped looking at her. He was just staring over her shoulder into the distance.

"Jed?" He looked back at her, his face a mask. "I need your help." It took a moment, but then the smile she loved crept back onto this face.

"I'll think about it," he said. She was hurt, a little, that he hadn't agreed right away. Though, she knew it sounded crazy. Maybe even Jed had his limits.

Jed checked his phone. "You have made us late. We can talk more at lunch. Now come on, my little subconscious warrior. Before we freeze our faces off."

* * *

During New World History, as Mr. Newsome droned on about the various interrelationships of the European ruling families during the Middle Ages, Finn started making a list of what she knew about Noah's travels and the connections with Sydney Norwich. Nothing new revealed itself as she made her lists. All she managed to do was not be paying attention when Mr. Newsome called on her with a question about Eleanor of Aquitaine. And the only reason she thought that was the question was because he'd written Eleanor's name on the whiteboard.

"Sorry, Mr. Newsome."

"It was in the reading before you got sick, Miss Driscoll."

Seth coughed, quietly. She glanced over at him. He had written *Henry II* in capital letters next to his row of numbers. *France* and *England* were below that, connected with an arrow. Finn turned back to the front of the room.

"I'm just a little foggy. Um . . . I think it's Henry the Second. And France . . . to England?"

"The uptick in your voice doesn't inspire confidence, but you're right."

Finn waited until Mr. Newsome went back to his whiteboard, and then she mouthed *Thank you* to Seth. He smiled. Whatever trauma she'd caused by popping into his dream, it seemed that he was over it.

Jed was waiting when she got to the cafeteria. Like he did every day, he checked her tray as she set it on the table. "You've got your appetite back."

She looked down at her tray. It was full of food.

When she looked back at him, he had that look on his face that he got when there was a new cool thing to be learned and mastered. "I'm in," he said.

"What if it's all in my head?"

"Then we have a funny story to tell later. What do you need me to do?"

Finn pulled Noah's notebook out of her bag.

"I want to find Noah."

"Got it. Save the little guy."

"I've been through his dream journal. Noah was on some sort of quest. To where or for what, I don't know. There are some symbols—a triangle-circle-square thing—and a labyrinth. But other than that . . . it's just an almost infinite world of possibilities."

"It's like a video game."

"Kind of."

He took the notebook and tucked it into his book bag.

When he turned back to her, she said, "I know you've got questions. Go ahead." His face lit up.

"So it's like having superpowers?"

"Not exactly." Finn explained the way the dream world worked, at least what she'd figured out so far and what Rafe had told her. Jed took it in, occasionally interrupting to compare it to some graphic novel or movie he loved.

"I want you to check out my dreams," he finally said when she finished.

"I'm not sure I should do that. I freaked Moby out."

"I'm not asking you to go in and help me slay a dragon. Just come look, and then we can talk about it the next day."

"Do you remember your dreams?"

"Not always, but if I don't, I don't. This is the only way to confirm it's really happening."

He was right about that. Jed picked up a french fry. "If all these dreams are like a river, could you walk backward in it to see a dream someone had in the past? Like the dream I had when I was seven about going to the center of the sun and discovering it was made of Gummi Bears?"

"I have no idea."

It was a question she'd never thought to ask. Jed was good at that kind of thinking. He shrugged and started to dig into his lunch. "It'd be way cool if you could."

The rest of the day passed in the normal way that school days do, some good moments, some not so good. In Algebra II, Jack Bliss, a boy who normally acted like the class was being conducted in a foreign language, successfully solved a quadratic equation. The rightness of his answer caught everyone by surprise. So much so that when Jack turned from the smartboard looking as if he'd just won a Nobel Prize, the class burst into applause. Diane Billingsley, the head cheerleader, even high-fived Jack as he walked back to his seat. "I don't know what happened. It just clicked" was all Jack could say.

That victory carried Finn all the way to her final class,

biology, when she turned a corner and saw Deborah Marks with her arms wrapped around Marcus outside the classroom. Right as the bell rang, Deborah whispered something in his ear, and Marcus blushed. Deborah took off down the hall; Marcus smiled and walked into the lab.

Finn realized there was a tight place in her chest.

Which didn't make any sense. Other than that one dissection, they barely interacted. They didn't text. They didn't sit next to each other in the cafeteria or study hall. She didn't know the names of his parents or if he had any siblings.

Why did Finn care if Marcus liked Deborah Marks?

The second bell rang. When it stopped, the sound of it kept bouncing around the empty hallway.

And Finn suddenly realized she didn't. She was just sad that high school was never going to be that for her. Even if she could get past the cloud of doom everyone saw floating over her, how could she focus on the sewing club (was there a sewing club and would they let her in even if she didn't know how to sew?) when she needed to save her brother?

She followed Marcus into the lab. She hoped he and Deborah were happy. And she hoped that someday she'd be happy like that, too.

ELEVEN

Finn forced herself to finish *Fahrenheit 451*. It was a great book, full of worthy thoughts and sympathetic, if flawed, characters. But she was happy to be done with it so she could write her paper. Mrs. Jepsen, her English teacher, felt bad about Noah. Finn knew that because she'd said it about a hundred times. She'd probably give Finn a pretty good grade even if she wrote a shitty paper, which was almost certain since her goal was writing fast, not making sense.

On the walk home from school, she and Jed had decided that he would focus on Noah's journal; she would focus on Sydney Norwich's memoir. Since she'd already read it, they thought it an efficient use of resources, but they were both also fairly certain he'd get bored in the middle.

Finn finished her paper in about an hour (she'd titled it "The Liberation of Censorship," hoping it sounded smart, even though Finn wasn't sure that the paper itself supported the provocative title), and then turned to the Internet. She'd already

searched for Sydney when she first read his book. There had
been a lot of Sydney Norwiches in the world, but none of them
were the one she was looking for. She didn't think she'd have
any better luck today, so instead she started researching Somersetshire, Sydney's home.

Somersetshire was by all accounts a beautiful place.
Green hills, lots of old buildings. People from the area
seemed unnaturally focused on a storm in 1703, which
destroyed the local church. But other than that . . . lots of
green hills and old buildings. Finn couldn't find any mention
of Dreamwalkers or magic. Or even "Magick," which is how
they sometimes spelled it back then. The only thing Finn found
that might be helpful was a nearby monastery known, then
and now, for its library. "Books left by travelers of all nations,"
someone said. Maybe there was something there that would
help. But how the hell was she going to get to a monastery in
England?

Before she could formulate an answer or even decide if it
was the right question, she heard a knock on her door. Finn
clicked to the web page she'd opened about Ray Bradbury and
mumbled, "Come in," pretending to be engrossed in the information in front of her as Nana entered the room.

"How's it going, sweetheart?" Finn turned around and
sighed when she saw the mug in Nana's hand. "Rafe called. He
said you were supposed to come over this afternoon."

Finn held up the printout of her report. "I had to finish
my paper." She heard how lame it sounded. Her brother's life

was at stake. "And . . . I don't think Rafe knows any more than you do."

"Still. Tomorrow you need to go to the gym." She held out the mug for Finn to take.

"I don't want any more of that."

Finn really didn't want to drink the sludge. But Nana had clearly been instructed to make sure she did. Nana smiled at her. "I know. I'll wash the mug for you. It's a sticky mess and you have enough to do."

Finn wasn't willing to fight about it.

She left a little in the bottom of the mug and didn't swallow her final mouthful. Nana didn't notice. She took the mug, kissed Finn on the cheek, and left. Finn almost gagged as she rushed to the garbage can to spit out what was still in her mouth. She quickly drank the glass of water by her bed. Maybe dilution would help.

Finn spent another hour searching for something . . . anything that might reveal what had ultimately defeated Sydney. She now knew a lot about mazes, black grouse, and fevers in the eighteenth century, but not anything that could be helpful. And, thanks to the mug of gunk Nana had given her, she was exhausted.

Finn lay down on top of her sheets. She wasn't sure what she planned to do. She wasn't sure what she could do. In his notebook, Noah never talked about being scared. Confused, yes, but never scared.

Finn was scared. What if she wasn't smart enough or strong enough to help Noah? What if she was too late and he was already lost? What if she wasn't going to get another good night's sleep for the rest of her life?

So far, being a Dreamwalker sucked.

She closed her eyes.

Finn heard movement in front of her, but it was so dark she couldn't see what it was. Shouldn't a Dreamwalker be able to get a little light in a room?

And just like that, the Lochran around her neck started to glow a little brighter, and Finn saw naked feet leading to naked legs; two bodies entwined on red sheets, faces hidden in the shadows.

A male hand traced a circle in the small of a woman's back.

Finn didn't want to be there, even if it was just a dream. She started to move back to the River when she heard a moan and, without thinking, turned toward it. The woman threw back her head into a shaft of moonlight that streamed through the window.

Finn was lying on the bed. Well, not Finn. A dreamed version of Finn, mostly like her but prettier and with fluffier hair. And, unlike the real Finn, naked and not alone. This couldn't be her own dream, could it? Was that even possible?

Her mind was suddenly blank, and she couldn't think of what to do next. She took a step back and bumped into a chair covered with clothes. It scooted into the wall with a thump.

"What was that?" she heard herself ask.

"Who cares?" the young man replied.

Jed.

Finn watched him lift himself up on his elbows, bringing his face into the moonlight. He was smiling. He looked happy.

This was Jed's dream.

Finn really needed to go. She closed her eyes.

"So where were we?" she heard Jed ask.

Why was she still here? Wake up! *she thought. It bounced like a scream around her head. She could hear Jed and Dream Finn kissing and laughing.*

Finn felt her heart beating in her chest.

She willed the sound to get louder so it would block out the noises in the room.

BA-BOOM, BA-BOOM, BA-BOOM.

"Yes, just like—"

Louder!

BA-BOOM, BA-BOOM, BA—

The sound vibrated through her whole body but didn't drown out a moan from the bed. Was that Jed or was it her? She didn't want to know. What the hell did she have to do to get out of here? Somewhere else, *Finn thought. And, unbidden, two more words:* Deborah Marks.

Then—

Silence.

She was in a long and thin room. It was still dark, except for a small doorway in the distance. The walls were unfinished and covered with pipes. Crouching behind a pipe, she saw a shadow.

Someone hiding. Finn took a step, and the shadow darted past her, knocking her over.

The "someone," Finn quickly realized, was a mouse, about the same size she was. And, just as quickly, she knew the mouse was Deborah Marks. Something about it, the eyes, the way it moved: It was Deborah in mouse form.

Finn followed Mouse Deborah toward the doorway, which was really a hole in the wall. Mouse Deborah skittered into a large room. She ran around the baseboard, avoiding a man and a woman who sat at a table covered in ashes. They were thin, with hollow eyes. The woman at the table saw Mouse Deborah scurrying across the room. "There she is. Get her wallet!"

Finn wondered why a mouse would have a wallet right as the man jumped up and stamped his foot, sending Mouse Deborah back the way she'd come. The woman grabbed a broom and swatted at the small creature as it darted back and forth, trying to avoid being caught or killed. "Give it to me!" the woman screamed.

Mouse Deborah chirped in response. Finn remembered she was a mouse, too. If she wanted to understand, she could—

"Mom. Please. I don't have any money," Finn heard Mouse Deborah say.

But the woman didn't understand or didn't care. The broom kept flying. Mouse Deborah's chirps became louder and more frightened.

Finn threw herself into the room. She saw her tiny mouse fingers on the floor. Her little legs churning as fast as they could toward the broom. Stop the broom.

"She brought a friend," the man said, pointing at Mouse Finn.

Deborah's mom swung the broom in Finn's direction. It hit her and knocked her across the floor. Finn looked around, saw Mouse Deborah huddled underneath a cabinet. Finn scrambled to her feet.

"Run!" she yelled, though the sound came out as some sort of squeak. But it worked. Mouse Deborah began running back toward the hole in the wall.

Finn moved toward the man and woman. The man stomped on Finn's tail. "Gotcha," he said. Finn's back burned from the pressure of her tail being pressed against the floor. Mouse Deborah disappeared into the wall as Deborah's mother raised her foot to crush Finn.

She's going to kill me, *Finn thought.* What happens then?

Above her, the foot started to come down.

I am not a mouse, *she remembered.* I am a Dreamwalker. *Finn stood up on her hind legs and stretched her front legs high in the air. The shoe hit her paw and—*

Finn woke up to someone whispering in her ear. She felt something wet hit her cheek.

"Good morning, sweetheart."

Finn saw her mother leaning over her, smiling and crying at the same time. How long had she been sitting there, watching Finn, waiting for her to wake up? Her mother leaned over and wrapped her arms around Finn, at least as much as she could, given that Finn was lying down.

After a moment, Finn hugged her back. What else could she do?

TWELVE

Finn expected her mother to have a thousand questions about Noah and Rafe and the dreams. But she didn't. She asked about school. And then, while Finn was getting dressed, her mom dug a beautiful Norwegian sweater out of her suitcase and gave it to her before they ate breakfast in Noah's room. When they were finished, Julia finally said, "I guess we should talk about your dreams."

Finn didn't really want to go through the whole story again. She wanted to tell her mother that she had it handled, that she should leave Finn and Nana to take care of it, just as they'd taken care of everything else. Before she could say any of that, though, she glanced toward the kitchen where Nana was listening. Nana gestured with her head toward Julia. *Tell her*, the gesture said.

Deep down, Finn knew that Nana was probably right. If only because her mom might be able to help.

"Noah's in my dreams," she finally said. "He's like a shadow of himself. Mostly Noah but not quite all there."

Finn looked at her brother. In the silence, Finn realized they'd all fallen into rhythm with his breathing.

"What did Rafe say?" her mother asked.

"I don't care. I don't trust him," Finn replied.

Julia turned to Nana in the kitchen. "But you do?"

"Yes. Because Noah did."

Julia nodded. After a moment, she stood up. "I guess we should talk to him."

Rafe offered to come to the house, but Julia wanted to go to the gym.

Finn and her mom were quiet as they walked to the car. It was only when they both ended up at the passenger side that Julia asked, "Have you been practicing your driving?"

"There aren't too many chances. Nana doesn't drive much, just to the market and stuff. And she does all that when I'm home to watch Noah."

Her mother handed her the keys. "No time like the present."

Finn didn't really want to drive. Her last experience had been horrible. Jed's father had let her drive through town and then tried to teach her to parallel park. But Jed was in the back seat making jokes, and she ended up driving onto the curb. So, as she put on her seat belt and adjusted her mirrors, she set "not crashing" as her goal. It was a low bar, but one she thought she could manage.

As they drove through town, she could see her mother

working an "invisible" brake, but Julia never corrected Finn or pointed out the obvious traffic dangers. Her mother passed the time by telling Finn about life in Norway and how the oil company had agreed to let her work from home for the foreseeable future.

"How long's 'foreseeable'?" Finn asked.

"I don't know. How long will it take to make sure you're safe?"

"Probably as long as it'll take me to pull into this parking spot."

Much to Finn's dismay, the only parking spot she'd found near the gym was a parallel spot between a large pickup truck and an expensive sports car. Whoever drove the pickup had made no effort to pull close to the curb.

"Do you want to do it?" Finn asked her mother.

"This is easier than anything you've been through in the last year."

And then, with a confidence that helped Finn understand how her mother thrived in an industry dominated by men who didn't want to listen to her, her mom deftly explained how to parallel park.

Pull up next to the pickup. Put the car in reverse. Look over her right shoulder. As Finn got even with the rear of the truck, her mother told her to turn the steering wheel to aim the back of the car into the spot, then when she'd cleared the truck, to turn it the other direction. Straighten out and, just like that, Finn was parked. Admittedly, farther away from the curb than she was supposed to be, but she was in the spot.

Finn turned the car off and opened the door. The roof light came on. Finn could see her mother's face reflected in the window in front of her.

"Did you think that Noah's coma happened because he was a Dreamwalker?"

"Only when the doctors couldn't find another cause."

"You should have stopped him."

Julia took the blow, then quietly said, "I didn't know how."

"It was your job to figure it out." The words came out louder than Finn had intended. She wasn't trying to pick a fight, she just didn't understand how all these adults, all these people who were supposed to love Noah and take care of him, how they let this happen.

Finn watched her mother's eyes darting back and forth, the way they did when she was thinking. Finally, they stopped. She reached out and touched Finn's cheek. Her hand was warm. Her fingers were soft. "I know. I'll do better this time."

When they got inside, Julia looked around, and Finn realized she didn't know where to go. "You've never been here before?"

"Rafe always picked Noah up. Or met us outside the gym."

"What was he hiding?"

"It didn't dawn on me that he was hiding anything."

As they walked across the gym, Finn explained the crazy stairs, and when they got to them, Julia leaned over and ran her hands along the top and bottom of the second stair. "The center has been shaved to less than a millimeter. It's not load-bearing at all."

"I think that's the point. You step there, you fall."

Finn watched her mother run her fingers around a hole in another step.

"And this has been buffed smooth by going with the grain. The only way to do that would be by hand. It would have taken forever."

Finn shrugged. "Just because they're homemade doesn't make him any less crazy." And, with that, she moved forward to guide her mother up to the top, one careful footstep at a time.

Rafe wasn't glad to see them. It wasn't anything he said or did. He smiled when he opened the door, offered them a seat on the couch and some tea, but Finn could feel it. Something was off. After a few minutes, she decided it was guilt. More than anyone, Rafe was responsible for what happened to Noah. He let everyone believe the training was making Noah safe. He let Noah believe he could do what needed to be done. He'd been wrong.

When they started talking about Finn's training, and Rafe's theory that Noah was reaching out for her help, stuff Finn already knew, she stopped paying attention. She walked over to his bookcases and scanned the titles, looking for anything else that might help the search for her brother. She found an old book with a bird on its spine and pulled it off the shelf, but it was written in some ancient language that seemed more picture than alphabet. If it were helpful, she'd never know it. As she slid it back into its place, she glanced at her mother. Julia smiled at her. Finn could see that it was taking all her Mom's willpower not to cry. Finn had been mad in the car, but, now, she couldn't hold on to it. She flashed back to her mother's dream . . .

What are you looking for? . . . You . . . I'm right here.

Finn felt the weight of her mother's dream tears on her shoulder.

Julia didn't want any of this to happen. But . . .

There was no way anyone could have stopped Noah. He was stubborn.

Maybe she and her mom should leave and go have breakfast, talk about school and boys and how cold it is in Norway. Finn was adrift in the list of things they could do to distract themselves when she heard her mom say, "Monastery." It turned out Julia had been searching all over Europe for information about Dreamwalkers. She'd gone to libraries, universities, rare booksellers, and monasteries, any place with old books that seemed promising. It was how she spent her free time.

Finn watched her mom reach into her purse and pull out a stack of papers. The pages had been folded and unfolded hundreds of times. "There was a ledger from a clerk in a small town in northern England," she said. "The early pages were lists of people's property: sheep, cows, rounds of cheese. But then it started to get more frenzied, scribbles all over, drawings of crazy things. Like Noah's journal." She couldn't photocopy the documents, so her mom had drawn them, replicating the frenzy as best as she could.

She held the pages out to Rafe, who cautiously took them, flipping through them as if they were dusted in poison.

"*Malum*," he said quietly.

"It was written over and over again." She paused. "I remembered it from Noah's journal. There must be a connection, right?"

"It's just a word." From the look on her mother's face, it was clear she didn't believe that. Finn certainly didn't. She doubted Rafe even believed what he was saying.

He handed the pages back to Julia, and she tucked them back in her purse.

"I'm not sure how they help."

"Rafe, you have to do something," Julia pleaded. "My son is dying, and my daughter is—"

She stopped, almost like she'd just remembered Finn was there. Finn looked between Rafe and her mother. Rafe saw her and looked away. Guilty. Why?

Did he know how to fix all this?

Did he know it couldn't be fixed?

Finn's eyes locked on the scar on Rafe's neck. Something clicked.

"Why can't you go into the River anymore, Rafe?" she demanded. Her mother looked at her, confused. Maybe surprised.

"I just can't."

"Dreamwalkers are born. You said the gift chooses you. Why don't you use your gift anymore? Why don't you—"

"Shut up, Finn." He leaped to his feet. His face was contorted with rage. "Just shut up!"

Finn shut up.

After a moment, he collapsed back onto the couch, his head in his hands.

It was the first moment since they'd met that Finn had actually liked him.

Finn and her mother sat there as Rafe struggled to control himself. His energy was sharp, anxious, but then slowly it evened out as he took some of the centering breaths he'd taught her the day before. In the silence, Julia reached out and took Finn's hand. Her mother's hands were cold.

Finally, Rafe lifted his head.

"Fifteen years ago, I died. Not figuratively. I died. I saw something in the dream world that scared me so much I ripped the Lochran from my neck. I didn't know how powerful the cord was, how connected to me it had become. When I pulled it off, it cut my carotid artery. I was engaged at the time, and my fiancée was a nurse. She saved me. Explaining how I'd gotten a life-threatening injury lying in bed was . . . harder."

"Like Sydney Norwich," Finn said.

"Yes." He rubbed the scar. To Finn's eye, it looked angrier than it had just a moment before.

"Why didn't you tell us?" Julia asked.

"I knew Noah wasn't going to stop, and I . . ." He paused a long time. "I thought maybe if I could help him, it would help me." Julia reacted, but Rafe jumped in before she could say anything. "I did try to help him. I did everything I could to get him to wait, to take the herbs. And when that didn't work, I tried to convince him it was okay to go into the River without actually helping people. I even called a Dreamwalker I know in Brazil to see if she could find Noah in the dream space and talk to him. But all he wanted to talk about was how he could be better, stronger. He wouldn't even consider stopping." Finn knew that side of Noah.

Rafe offered Julia a sad smile. "I also knew that if I told you my story, you'd just worry more than you were already worrying." He smiled at her. There was a kindness to it. Maybe this was the side of him that Noah saw.

Julia looked at Finn and then at Rafe. "I guess you should tell us everything. But maybe some tea first."

Rafe followed Julia to the kitchen. Finn could hear them whispering and assumed it was about whether he should tell Finn the truth or not about what happened to him. Finn could tell by Julia's tone that she was being insistent. At one point she pretended to look at a book on the bookshelf to get closer, but they stopped talking. Her mom came out of the kitchen with tea and something like a smile.

They all sat down on the couch. Julia and Rafe on either side of Finn.

Rafe handed her a notebook and a ballpoint pen. "Take notes, ask questions at the end. Once I get started, don't interrupt me, or I might not want to keep going." He waited for Finn to open the notebook and click the end of her pen.

And once he started talking, the words flooded out of him.

* * *

Rafe's mother died when he was twelve. When he turned sixteen, there was no one to help him understand what was happening in his dreams. It was only years later, when he found a stack of letters belonging to his mother hidden in an old piece of furniture, that he discovered she'd had the gift, too.

He'd wandered through the River for years, popping in and out of people's dreams and nightmares without thinking he should help them or having any fear that he might harm them. Until the day he found himself in the middle of a war. A battle between a small group of men and women and an army of creatures from every myth he'd ever read. Rafe stayed on the fringes until one of the creatures attacked him. A woman ran over and defended him. She screamed at him, "Dreamwalker, draw your sword!" And when Rafe looked down, he realized he had a sword. He joined the battle. Ultimately, the creatures retreated, and almost immediately, the Dreamwalkers disappeared, called to their own dawns or destinies. Rafe was left with real-life cuts and bruises and even more questions. From that day, he decided to figure out what a Dreamwalker was and how he could do it better than anyone else.

"All these books," Rafe said, looking around the room, "helped me understand how I was supposed to do it." He traveled around the world to find other Dreamwalkers and learn from them. It became his calling. He worked to be the best, most powerful version of himself. He devoted his energy to helping people in their dreams. He wanted to make their lives better, make the world better.

It gave his life purpose.

"Until . . ."

It hung there. Just like with Noah, something had gone wrong.

Rafe had been helping an older woman. She reminded him of his mother. Over a series of weeks, she was trapped in a recurring nightmare: accused of being a witch by villagers with torches, who held dogs that pulled at their leashes, eyes flashing fire. The woman was dragged from her house and tortured.

Each night, Rafe bravely tried to help her. On most nights, he failed. Arriving too late, or unable to vanquish the crowds. He spent his waking hours trying to find her so he could understand why it was happening. He grew tired and weak. His fiancée begged him to go to a doctor, to get help. Rafe knew he should stop, but he couldn't let the old woman down. He kept trying to help.

Until that final night.

He arrived at the old woman's dream home and found it empty. For a brief moment, Rafe thought she'd been saved. But then he heard the villagers. They were outside, screaming for him to come out.

It confused Rafe that the dream existed even though the old woman wasn't there, but he decided to confront her tormentors, in case this was some kind of remnant emotional experience. He went outside. The dream was different from the ones before. The villagers were strong. And there were so many of them, more than he'd seen in any of the other dreams. He fought and fought, ultimately realizing he was going to lose. He tried to flee, to escape the dream. But he couldn't. He couldn't get back to the River.

The villagers carried him to a stake in the middle of a pile of branches. They tied him to it, and one of them held up a flaming torch.

It was the old woman.

Rafe realized that he hadn't been walking in her dream. These had been his dreams. She was his creation. He was attacking himself. He had no idea how he'd been wrong all that time, no idea how he'd allowed it to happen. It was like he'd been conned, but somehow he'd conned himself.

None of his research had prepared him for anything like this. He was trapped. And then, when the woman set the torch to the pile of wood, it started to burn, and the heat felt real. As the flames surged, the old woman laughed. The pain from the fire was worse than anything he'd ever felt. He kept pulling against the ropes and eventually got one hand free. And with the smell of his own burning flesh in his nose, he tore the Lochran from his neck and . . .

Darkness.

He woke up a week later in the hospital.

"I haven't had a dream since," he said. "Sleep is . . . a void. It's not restful or restless. It's just the time between closing my eyes and opening them again. But the world . . . it's less vibrant somehow. I don't know if it's the lack of dreams or what I went through. But it's like I live in a fog. If I had it to do over again, I think . . . I would have let the fire burn. I might have died, but maybe . . ."

He wouldn't have died, Finn thought. He would have lapsed into a coma he couldn't wake up from. Finn knew her mother was thinking the same thing, because Julia turned away from her. Finn wished she could say something that would let her mother know everything was going to be okay, but what exactly would she say? *"It's okay, Mom. Noah's not dead. He's just being burned at the stake. Or whatever his version of torture is."* No way that helped.

But there must be some way to use Rafe's experience.

"Who was the old woman?" Finn asked.

Rafe shrugged. "I don't know. In all the dreams where I was trying to help her, she felt like my mother, smelled like my mother. Or what I remembered her smelling like. Vanilla. But at the end, it was clear she was just evil. Even with the fire burning around me, I felt a coldness coming from her."

Finn flashed back to her dream the night before. The "hole" she'd reached into. The chill. A space empty of goodness.

Finn had touched that void and survived.

That had to mean something.

Out of the corner of her eyes, she saw her mother turn toward them. Julia's eyes were bright. She'd been crying. Finn put a hand on her mother's leg. "I've got this, Mom."

Finn looked at Rafe's library. "Which of these are your Dreamwalking journals?"

Rafe shook his head. "Come on, Rafe," Finn insisted. "Dreamwalking nerd like you? You wrote down everything. I know you did. And I get that they're personal. But give them to me anyway. You owe us that."

It took a long time, but Rafe eventually crossed to the shelves and grabbed a handful of books. He carried them over to Finn and Julia. Julia reached out, but Rafe didn't hand them over right away.

"I'm sorry, Julia. I really tried to help him."

Her mom took the books.

"Rafe," Finn said. "You knew that ripping the Lochran would get you expelled from the dream world. Sydney Norwich talks about it. So why did you do it?"

"I'm not sure." Rafe thought for a long moment. "I don't have the perfect recall I used to. But I think the old woman told me to. I think she said it would end my pain." It was clear from the way he said it that he'd simply traded one kind of pain for another.

Julia reached up and put a hand on his arm. Rafe looked at her hand but said nothing. After a moment, he turned and walked away. He headed through a door Finn had never noticed. The edge of it fit seamlessly into the wall. When he closed the door behind him, it was as if the door disappeared. It was as if Rafe had disappeared.

Finn assumed he'd gone into his bedroom.

She imagined a bed, a lamp, a nightstand covered with books.

A place to wait for morning.

To remember the dreams that were and mourn the ones never to be.

THIRTEEN

Finn drove. Her mother looked out the window. They were almost home when her mom said, "Your father was a Dreamwalker," so quietly Finn barely heard it.

"I thought he might be."

Out of the corner of her eye, Finn saw her mother turn toward her. "Why?"

"Nana said it runs in families and, based on that family tree Nana showed me, our branch of the clan definitely pulled the short straw." Her mom nodded, whether because of her good guess or the "short straw," Finn didn't know.

Finn stopped behind a delivery truck at a red light. "I saw Dad in one of my first Dreamwalker dreams," she said quietly. "At least, it looked like him. How I remember him."

"It wasn't your father."

Finn didn't want the cold, cruel man she'd seen to be her father. "Maybe people exist in the dream space even after they die," she said.

Julia shook her head. "Your dad tore his Lochran when you were born. He said he didn't want being a Dreamwalker to interfere with being a father. Sydney Norwich, Rafe, everything I've learned since Noah went into his coma says the same thing: Lose your Lochran, walk no more."

"Don't you wonder about where it all came from?"

"No. I just want to know how to stop it from afflicting my children."

Finn pulled into the driveway and turned off the ignition.

"What's next?" her mother asked.

Finn knew exactly what she had to do. Sydney and Rafe had been expelled from the dream world when they ripped their Lochrans. Finn was confident her brother had refused to do that. He'd been captured, wounded, trapped, but Finn knew he was still in the dream space. All she had to do was find him and bring him home.

And she had all the pieces she needed—Noah's journals, Sydney's book, Rafe's notes—she just had to figure it out. Jed would help her.

She felt bad keeping secrets from her mom, but she didn't have a choice.

Julia's job was to make sure Finn was okay. Finn's job was to save Noah. Those two things might not be compatible.

Finn looked at her mother, who was waiting for an answer to her question. She could see the fear in her eyes. Finn opened her eyes a little bit to give her answer that ring of truthfulness. "I think I'd like to go to school."

* * *

Finn took the monastery notes out of her mother's purse. *Stole* might be a better word, but Finn decided taking it fit into the "greater good" category. She also pocketed one of Rafe's journals. Mom would definitely notice if she took all of them.

When she got to school—with a note that she'd had an appointment—she took the long way to English class so she could go by fifth-period physics. Jed had it, and she thought she might be able to catch his eye. She'd sent him a text this morning: *Mom home. Can't walk.* He'd written back, *Good for you. Bad for Jed.* As much as Finn was leery about seeing him after walking into his dream the night before, she was certain he'd been up much of the night thinking about Noah's journal and the maze. And chances were, he'd found something. That's what Jed did.

If he asked if she'd gone into his dreams, she was going to lie. It was easier.

She stood at the door to his class, trying to get his attention, while staying out of the teacher's line of sight. Jed was doodling, which probably looked like note-taking to the teacher. Keisha Williams, who sat two rows in front of him, saw Finn. It took a long pantomime for Finn to communicate she wanted Jed. When Keisha finally realized what Finn wanted, she ripped a small corner of her notebook, wadded it up, and threw it at him. Jed looked up, annoyed, but his annoyance turned to delight when Keisha pointed at the door.

He immediately went back to his notebook and started

writing. After a moment, he held up a scribbled sign: *I figured it out!*

There were only two periods left in the day, but Finn was finding it hard to concentrate. What had Jed figured out? Would it be enough to help her find Noah? She pulled her mother's monastery notes out of her backpack and studied them while Mrs. Hewitt talked about a system of linear inequalities at the board. It was easy to see why her mother had found the original document compelling. Based on her notes, it had the same energy as Noah's journal at the end. No maze, but several references to birds and water.

Finn looked up. Deborah Marks sat several rows in front of her. She was playing with her hair, twirling it around her finger, which pulled it away from the back of her neck. Right below her hairline, Finn saw a yellow splotch, like a bruise that was halfway healed.

A weird place for a bruise.

Unless someone grabbed you around the neck.

On Fridays, Finn had study hall for her final period. She often skipped it and went home. No one in the office gave her any trouble, since they knew she was helping to take care of Noah. But today she had to wait for Jed, and she knew Marcus had last-period study hall, too. Even if they weren't really friends, Deborah had always been nice to Finn. Finn would never forgive herself if something bad happened to Deborah and she hadn't tried to help. Right now, she didn't have any proof that something was going on: just a dream and a bruise. Marcus might tell her something, though, if she could figure out how to ask him.

She looked around. He was sitting by himself at a table in the back.

Finn walked by six empty tables to get to him. She pulled out some homework and sat down, offering him a quiet "Hi" as she did. Marcus looked around, clearly noticing how many other tables she could have chosen to sit at.

He had a notebook open in front of him, an old-fashioned ballpoint in his hand. Finn didn't see the novel on the table, but she guessed he was working on his *Fahrenheit 451* paper, which was due Monday. He'd stopped writing in the middle of a sentence.

She flipped through her notebook, but she was really watching Marcus out of the corner of her eye. He was staring at the page like he hoped the words would appear by themselves. *Daydreaming*, Finn thought.

She closed her eyes, hoping she was right, that the stream of subconscious that connected our dreams, Rafe's "axis mundi," might keep flowing even if we were awake. She heard the *tick, tick, tick* of a clock on the back wall. She focused on it, took a deep breath . . . waited.

And then . . .

The now-familiar cacophony of sounds, all the dreams merging together in the flow of images, emotions. More beautiful than she remembered. She tried to sense Marcus, to see if his daydreams had brought him here. She heard someone singing—

And opened her eyes.

Saw a dragon.

A woman with eight arms.

A rainbow made only of red and purple stripes.

Marcus, *she thought again.*

Something crashed against her leg. She jumped away from it and came down in—

A long hallway.

Each one of a thousand linoleum tiles a different color, making an enthusiastic checkerboard. An empty checkerboard. It didn't seem like a setting for any dream of Marcus's, but maybe she didn't give him enough credit. She heard footsteps behind her and turned around. There he was . . .

Naked, except for socks and running shoes. Finn looked away. Why the hell was everyone naked?

Marcus approached her. Stopped. "I'm late for class," he said.

Finn almost laughed. Marcus was in the middle of a "naked at school" and "late to class" nightmare combo. The English paper was scaring him. She took off the jacket she was wearing and handed it to him. He started to put it on.

"I think maybe tie it around your waist," she offered.

Only then did he notice he was naked. He blushed and covered himself with the jacket. "Which way to Mrs. Jepsen's class?"

"Are you late for English, Marcus?"

He nodded.

"You know," Finn said, "I think one of the most interesting things in Fahrenheit 451 is the role of women. The girl is the instigator. The old woman dies for her convictions. His wife can't relate to his strug-gle." Finn wondered if technically this was cheating. *"But the book allows for a lot of different interpretations. Whatever interests you is as valid as what interests anyone else."*

Finn's words echoed down the hallway. She waited until there was silence. "Deborah needs you, Marcus." He looked at her intently. "Find out what's wrong. Help her." She didn't know how, but she felt that he understood what she was saying. She pointed down the hall. "See if your class is that way."

He headed off. Finn closed her eyes and . . .

Became aware of the *tick, tick, tick* of the clock.

Finn opened her eyes. Marcus was still sitting beside her, ballpoint still poised over the paper. "I think it's great you and Deborah are together," she said, hoping to drive home her sub-conscious idea. Marcus stared at her like she was crazy. Maybe she was. She pressed on. "I mean, it's great that she's got you to talk to about, you know, everything." *Everything?* Finn realized that it was both too vague and too specific. "It just seems like she's got a lot going on. And you're a good listener. And kind." She pointed at his paper. "Like Guy Montag. You're affected by what happens to people. You want to help them."

Marcus was looking through her. She stood up. "Anyway. Have a great evening." He didn't respond. He had already started writing furiously. She threw her backpack over her shoulder. She'd helped him with his paper. It made her optimistic about the rest of it.

Jed was waiting outside for her after school, bouncing from one foot to the other. Finn thought he was cold, but it turned out he was just excited. He handed her a piece of paper. "The maze doesn't have a solution. If you were a rat looking for cheese through that bottom door, you'd die of starvation."

Finn took the page. It was a photocopy of the maze from Noah's journal. Jed had used different colored pens to follow the complicated paths through it. Every color led to a dead end. No path led to the bottom exit. Only one path led to the center.

"The 'vile enigma,'" he said with a smile.

"I have no idea what that means," Finn answered.

"I found it online. From a poem about a guy who develops an elaborate maze and promises great riches to whoever can solve it. In the end, the person trying to solve it loses everything and no longer wants the riches."

They stood in silence. A wind blew, creating a chilling swirl around them.

Finn looked at him, trying to gauge if there was any weirdness. He waited, expecting her to say something, and when she didn't, Jed took the page back and looked at it. "I think the little man thought this maze was going to take him somewhere. Somewhere worth going."

Jed didn't do "layers." If he had a problem with you, you

knew it. He didn't remember his dream from last night. Finn was certain. And relieved.

She pointed at the bottom of the maze. "How did he know what the maze looked like? There's no way through it, yet he drew an exit at the bottom. But, based on what you've done, there's no way to get to the exit."

"Huh. I hadn't thought about that. I suppose he could've drawn it wrong, which invalidates my current theory. A depressing development, since I didn't pay attention during any of my morning classes while I was working on—"

"Hold on."

Finn unzipped her backpack and pulled out Sydney Norwich's book. She flipped to the maze page and laid Jed's photocopy over it.

Jed looked over her shoulder. "They're identical."

"The drawing wasn't a mistake. It's a trap. Someone gives you the map, and you go in, thinking it leads you through. Instead, they catch you."

"Who? The boogeyman?" He laughed. He meant it as a joke.

"*Malum*," she whispered. She could still feel the eel's teeth pinching her elbow: the searing pain, the cold. She thought it was just the little girl's nightmare. But now she knew it was something else, something deep and old and—

"Finn?"

Finn looked at Jed. He wasn't bouncing anymore. What she saw in his eyes was concern. She smiled, hoping to lighten the mood. "Yeah?"

"Who's 'Malum'? You mentioned him before."

Finn stamped her feet and blew into her gloves, pretending she was cold, just to buy a moment or two. How much truth was too much? "I'm not sure," she finally said.

"Remember when we did that Internet research on reading people's body language?" She did. She and Jed spent an entire afternoon trying to fool each other about what was true and what wasn't. She'd laughed so hard she'd fallen off the couch.

"When people lie," he reminded her, "they fidget and touch their mouths, both of which you just did."

"I'm not lying."

"You're not telling the truth."

Jed was the best person Finn knew. Good and kind and smart. Why couldn't she just tell him the truth?

He moved closer. "I get it. This is scary. Dangerous, even. There's some weird supervillain, which makes perfect sense because every superhero needs a nemesis."

"I'm not a superhero," Finn said quietly.

"That's what a superhero would say. Until they get comfortable with their cape or big hammer or put on their indestructible super smart suit."

"Again, I have no idea what you're talking about."

"Superman. Thor. Iron Man." Jed took Finn's face in his hands. "Whatever it is, I'm going to help you. Call me a sidekick if you have to. I prefer 'boy genius,' but that's not important. What's important is . . ."

He kissed her. His lips were warm, the skin of his face cold. She remembered the dream from the night before.

Jed liked her.

She felt Jed's lips pull away from hers, but he was so close all she could see were his eyes. They were smiling.

Finn burst into tears.

It took a while before she calmed down enough to explain that she wasn't crying because he kissed her. She was crying because . . . well, she wasn't exactly sure why she was crying. Sometimes Finn thought she was on the verge of tears all the time. Maybe when Jed kissed her, she was just too overwhelmed to keep it together. Or maybe she was crying . . . because it felt good not to be alone right now.

Or maybe she was crying because it would be nice to have a boyfriend and walk around school holding hands. That would feel normal. That would make high school . . . fun. But now, there wasn't time for fun because she had to huddle over old manuscripts to figure out what sort of evil was lurking in the axis mundi.

Or it was all of those. Or none of them.

Jed looked at her, expectantly.

He had little flecks of brown in his eyes.

Telling him why she was crying wasn't important.

What was important was getting out of the cold before her face froze. And figuring out what she was going to do tonight when she stepped into the River. Finally, she just said, "You're going to have to trust me. I'm not upset you kissed me. But I also can't think about you kissing me right now or I'll cry again."

"I'm going to take that as a good sign, even though I think a more logical person probably wouldn't."

Jed put an arm around her. She wasn't sure how to tell him she wasn't ready to go public as a couple, but it turned out he was just reaching for her backpack. She let him take it.

As they slowly walked home, Jed asked her what they should do now.

"You've helped. A lot. What you figured out about the maze, it makes me think that someone was after Noah. And that other guy, Sydney, maybe even Rafe."

"Why?"

"No idea. I also don't know what ties them together. Other than they're all Dreamwalkers."

"Which seems like a big thing."

"Yeah. I guess. Whoever, whatever, is doing this . . . they're smart and dangerous, and they've been hurting people for hundreds of years. At least."

"How does that help?"

"I know to be extra careful."

"Can I have the old book?"

It made sense to give all the material to Jed, but . . .

"Where are you with school?" Finn asked.

"Passing all my classes."

"Barely or by a comfortable margin?"

"State-school-acceptance comfortable."

This was one of Jed's few strict rules. He let himself goof off as much as he wanted as long as he was doing well enough to get into a good state college. If he went to a party school, he wanted it to be by choice.

"Okay, then. Go ahead and take it," she told him. "There's another journal in my backpack from Rafe, as well, and some notes my mom made at a monastery."

Jed reached into Finn's backpack. As he rummaged around, he said, "We're going to need to talk about it."

She knew what he meant. It wasn't the journals or the Dreamwalking.

"I know. Just not now."

"I think I get one question."

Finn nodded.

"Scale of one to ten, with ten being a certainty, what are the chances that I'll get to kiss you again?"

They had arrived at Jed's house. He tucked all the Dreamwalking materials under his arm and zipped up her backpack before handing it back.

Finn took the backpack and looked at him, his wide smile. All those days they walked to school, walked home. How many of those days had he wanted to kiss her? Finn's chest felt warm, like her heart had melted. She'd read that in books but didn't know what it meant. Now she did.

She stood on her tiptoes and kissed him.

"Ten," she said.

She turned for home. She didn't hear his footsteps. He was standing watching her.

"So definitely more after that one? Or was that one the one guaranteed by your ten?" he shouted.

Finn threw an arm up and waved goodbye.

"I'll text you if I find anything." And with that, she heard Jed's footsteps fade away as he ran toward home.

FOURTEEN

Her mom and Nana were sitting at the kitchen table when Finn walked in. A delicious smell hit her: chicken potpie, Finn's favorite.

"How was school?" her mother asked.

"Distracting."

All the Dreamwalker materials were on the table. Except for the ones Finn had already taken.

"Here are the rest," her mother said.

"I needed something to do in study hall."

"Are you going to tell us anything?" Nana asked.

Finn looked between them. She knew how hard this was. "Probably not."

Nana tried to make small talk during dinner, but Finn and her mother couldn't get with the flow. Eventually, Nana stopped, and they ate their chicken potpie in silence. When Finn had eaten as much as she could, which was a lot more than she actually wanted, she looked up and blurted out, "Jed kissed me."

Her mother's eyes went wide. Nana smiled. "I wondered when he was going to get around to it."

"How did I not know he liked me?" Finn asked.

"You weren't looking," Nana told her.

Finn's mother seemed caught between conflicting emotions. Eventually, she said, "That's great, honey. I guess the timing seems . . ."

"Off. I know. The reason I'm telling you is that, well, I haven't really had a boyfriend since Tommy McGill in third grade and I think having one would be really fantastic. Which means that I need to not get hurt or end up—" She tipped her head toward Noah's room. "I'm going to be safe, smart. Do what needs to be done and then come home and go to the prom."

"The prom's in three months," Nana said.

"You know what I mean. I just . . . I don't want you to worry."

Her mother reached out and took her hand.

"I hate to fall back on clichés, but as they say, that's what mothers do."

"It's not going to help."

"No, but everybody needs to feel like they're doing something, right?"

Finn scooted her chair back, ready to get up and get on with it. Except her mother wouldn't let go of her hand. "You're quite a young woman, Finn."

"Yes. I am. If by that you mean completely overmatched for the task at hand in almost every way."

Her mother and Nana laughed.

"My plan is to save Noah and then go back to being ordinary. Okay?"

They nodded. After a few moments, her mother said, "Your plan's a little short on details."

"It's a work in progress."

Finn headed to her room and threw herself on the bed almost at the same moment that her phone buzzed.

Jed.

Call me. ASAPASAPASAP.

She put in an earbud and hit speed dial two. He started talking without any warm-up pleasantries.

"Did you notice the thing in the middle of Sydney Norwich's maze?"

"The triangle in the circle in the square thing?"

"Do you know what that is?"

"I looked online. I didn't find anything just like it, but it resembles the alchemical symbol for—"

"The philosopher's stone," they said in unison.

Finn could tell that Jed was excited. When he got like that, he was incapable of letting people finish their sentences. "Turning lead into gold," he said. "Or a source of enlightenment. Or the elixir of life, enabling someone to live forever."

Finn interrupted. "It's just a story, Jed. No one ever found it. Ever. In the history of time, ever."

"But what if someone did? What if it's not in this world? What if living forever in this life isn't possible—"

She knew what he was thinking and finished his sentence. "But living forever in the dream world is."

"The guy Sydney Norwich was chasing—Peter. His wife was scared he was up to no good. And he was, but he wasn't a Dreamwalker. He didn't have one of those glowy necklaces. How did he do it?" Finn did not have an answer to that question, so Jed just kept plowing through his theory. "Maybe someone, someone who has the philosopher's stone, gave him that power so he could go around being awful in people's dreams, and then he'd wake up and be awful in the real world, too."

Goosebumps prickled Finn's skin. "The bad guy needs soldiers. To do all his bad things."

"Yes. What did you say?" Jed asked. "Before I kissed you."

"*Malum.*"

"Latin for 'evil,' right?"

He'd looked it up, knew exactly what they were dealing with. He didn't say anything for a long moment. Finn heard him exhale, then say, "I think you and Noah have stepped into some deep shit."

Finn took Jed's copy of the maze and tucked it into her pocket before she lay down on her bed. She'd need a weapon.

Dreamwalker Wan had that big sword. She'd need to get herself a big sword.

Or a spear, she thought as she closed her eyes. *Or a machete. Like it matters. I don't really know how to use any of them.* She could feel her pulse in the vein at the side of her neck. All that blood moving through her body. Round and round, twisting through veins and arteries and capillaries. How strange.

Ba-boom. Ba-boom. Ba-boom. BA-BOOM.

Finn heard the sound of a heartbeat. But it wasn't hers.

It was coming from the River of Dreams flowing around her. The heart was beating at the same rate as hers, like they were connected, but Finn didn't feel compelled to follow the sound. There was no menace in it. The dreamer felt no danger, and the sound got quieter as the River carried it away.

Finn took a moment, felt the energy of the dreams. There was the usual swirl of shapes and colors and smells and sounds. Each separate and yet mixed up in a great symphony.

She pulled the copy of the maze out of her pocket. In the background, she heard the sound of a storm. It passed by her feet, and she felt a charge of electricity. It didn't call to her, but the shock suddenly brought to mind something Jed had asked. Could she walk back through the River to the past, to dreams long since dreamed and forgotten?

For the first time, Finn turned around and looked at where the dreams were going. Unlike a real river, there was no horizon. The crush of it continued forever. But as the River moved off, the colors became more muted, eventually fading to black-and-white—except for a few spots that still blazed brightly. Are they fading as they become less visceral, forgotten, less emotionally charged? And, if that were true, what were the bright spots?

Only one way to find out.

She started downriver, walking at first, and then when the River put up no resistance, she broke into a run.

"I'm on my way, Noah," she said, comforted by the sound of her own voice. "I'm on my way."

FIFTEEN

In a place that was darker than dark, Noah stirred.

SIXTEEN

Finn ran, catching glimpses of grayscale dreams as she looked right and left. She wondered what effect, if any, she could have on dreams that had already been dreamed.

In the distance, the bright patch of color got no closer. She stopped, and the River quickly pushed the colors even farther away. Of course, she realized, there are always new dreams, pushing the old ones into the past.

She remembered a biology class she'd had last spring. They'd gone on a field trip to the river and studied water patterns. It had been surprisingly interesting, how the river made waves in the obstacles that it ran across, waves that bounced into one another, creating bigger waves or canceling each other out and creating patches of calm. The water kept moving, creating more and more activity, all governed by the same rules. "Fluid dynamics" is what she remembered her teacher calling it.

Obviously, the River of Dreams was different. The dreams weren't water, and Finn wasn't a rock. These were people's experiences, and she was . . .

What was she?

Finn reached out her hands and felt the dreams flow over her, almost through her. What was she? At home, she was just Finn. Not the girl she wanted to be or the almost-adult she sometimes pretended to be.

But who was she really?

Being a Dreamwalker was the path to finding her brother. Maybe it was also the path to waking up and finding herself. Here she could do anything.

Finn looked at the bright spot in the River now farther away than ever. I don't have to chase it, *she thought.* I'm already there.

She reached for the bright patch of dream, and as she did, she watched her arm stretch out like rubber, pulling her into a thin thread of Finn-ness and then—

Found herself in her own bedroom.

Sort of.

It was her room if it were dropped in the middle of a video game about the Middle Ages. And she was on the bed, eyes closed.

Or at least a dreamed version of herself was near the bed. Dream Finn was actually floating about two inches off the mattress.

Finn walked over to the bedside table. A paperback copy of Romeo and Juliet *was open on it and, next to the play, a piece of paper. Finn watched as words magically appeared on the paper. Her term paper was writing itself.*

She'd read the romance in freshman English. The teacher had forced them to read aloud every day. Some days, boys played girls and girls played boys, some days only the boys read, some days only the girls. After they'd finished the play, the teacher had brought actors into the class to read the important scenes. It changed everything. It was as if they'd been reading a different book all those weeks.

Finn reached down to pick up the book but couldn't. She yanked on it, but the book stuck stubbornly to the side table. She reached for the term paper. Same thing.

What the hell?

And then she realized what was happening: This dream was bright in the River because it was her dream. But it had already been dreamed, like a movie that had already been shot. It couldn't be changed, even by a Dreamwalker. She leaned over to look at her term paper.

It was writing about a speech of Mercutio's from Act I:

> True, I talk of dreams,
> Which are the children of an idle brain,
> Begot of nothing but vain fantasy,
> Which is as thin of substance as the air
> And more inconstant than the wind, who woos—

Finn hadn't written her paper on that part of the play. Why was she writing about dreams? Had she somehow known—

"I don't want to wake you, Finn."

Startled, Finn turned around.

"Noah!" He stood in the doorway. Around his neck, his Lochran glowed with a green light. She saw the handle of a sword sticking out over his shoulder.

Before she could do anything, the room began to break apart.

"No!" she screamed, but with a WHOOSH Noah disappeared, along with everything else.

Her scream echoed over blackness and then—

Finn woke up, a real scream trapped in her throat. She held it in, shaking.

SEVENTEEN

Noah had been here in the darkness a long time with only the silence to keep him company. But now, he felt something. Not the cold that tried to reach inside him to make him forget, but something else. Something warm that did not want to hurt him.

EIGHTEEN

Finn and Jed decided to get hot chocolate at a nearby coffee shop so they could talk without Finn's mom and grandmother listening in. As they walked, she recapped what had happened the night before.

"I mean, I didn't even remember the dream at the time. But now I totally remember the night I had it. It was raining. We were in the den. I was stressing out because I had to finish my paper, and I was flipping through *Romeo and Juliet*, trying to find a quote to match my theme. I read passages aloud while he played some game about a guy in a brown tunic—"

"*Assassin's Creed*. Two, three. Maybe four . . ." Finn glared at him. "I guess the number of the game is not important."

"Anyway. Noah told me he thought it was a dumb play, at least from a feminist perspective. And he went on some rant about suicide and the literary elite's attempt to redefine it as a female empowerment technique."

"That is not a thing."

"I don't know if it's a thing. He was ranting and talking to the video game at the same time, so I couldn't really follow. And I didn't really care, because I was trying to finish a paper for the next day's English class." Finn blew into her glove-covered hands to warm her lips. She should have worn a scarf. "But the dream has to be related, because it was sort of a jumbled mix of his video game and my stress about the paper."

Jed took it in for a moment and then said, "So the brighter parts of the old River are dreams you've already dreamed."

"I guess."

"And in this one you were dreaming about Noah?"

"No. The whole dream looked like the video game: brown with sharp edges. Even me hovering over the bed. Noah didn't, though. He looked like Noah. I think Noah the Dreamwalker walked into my dream, just like I've walked into other people's. He became a part of it."

"Why?"

"I don't know. I freaked out and woke up."

Jed walked along, his hands tucked into his pockets. Finn watched him out of the corner of her eye. His eyelashes were impossibly long. After a few moments, where the only sound was that of the snow crunching under their feet, he nodded in understanding.

"So Noah's doing his Dreamwalker thing and pops into your dream. Eavesdropping, sort of."

"Or he was trying to help me with something."

"Like what? Further development of his feminist theory

of *Romeo and Juliet*?" He smiled. "Which reminds me, did you check out my dream?"

Finn felt herself blush. She put her hands up to her cheeks to cover it.

"No," she lied. "I didn't get a chance."

"So we still don't know if you're crazy."

She quickly changed the subject. "Do you think Noah wanted to talk about what was going on with him?"

"There is only one way to know for sure."

She'd already thought of it. "I woke up before the dream was over. I should go back and find out."

"Exactly. But drop into my dream first. Okay?"

"Okay."

He hip-checked her slightly, throwing her sideways. When she caught her balance and looked at him, he was smiling. She blushed again, but this time she didn't try to hide it.

NINETEEN

School on Monday was unremarkable: a discussion about Ray Bradbury that convinced Finn half her English class hadn't read the book, a litany of boring facts about English kings and queens, and a PE class committed to putting young adults off exercise forever. What was more unsettling was that Deborah was absent. Could be that cold and flu season had gotten the best of her, but... there didn't seem to be a lot of other students out of school. Finn said a silent prayer to whatever god was listening that her stepping into Deborah's dreams hadn't harmed her in any way.

In biology, she asked Marcus how Deborah was, and he answered with a short "Fine," then ignored Finn for the rest of class. This did not inspire confidence in Deborah's "fine-ness."

As she and Jed walked home, it was clear the Dreamwalking world had filled most of their respective days. Jed was full of ideas. "You should reach out to some other Dreamwalkers, like that lady with the sword."

"I've considered it. But what if I contact a Dreamwalker Rafe knows and they tell him what I'm doing? He will not be happy to find out I'm going to follow Noah into his coma world with no idea how I'll find it, save him, or escape."

"What's he going to do, send you to your dream room?"

"Turn Nana on me. She'll be sneaking herb goo everywhere. I'll be sound asleep twenty-four seven. They will never let me dream again. At least, they'll try."

"I agree. That's why you should let *me* dream walk with you."

"That's completely nuts, and I doubt possible."

"Sure it is."

"Based on ... ?"

"That evil dude, Peter, in Norwich's book. He wasn't a Dreamwalker, right?"

"Norwich didn't think so."

"Yet, he was walking around in the dream space, making mischief, doing things he shouldn't be able to do."

"Okay ..."

"So, why can't I do the same, without the mischief?"

Classic Jed. An interesting question that created more questions, with an equal likelihood of being the right answer or a complete disaster.

"Because I have no idea how to do it. Norwich didn't say, and, if you'll recall, I'm a newbie."

"We agreed you would walk into my dream tonight, right?"

She had no intention of going into his dreams, but she wasn't going to tell him that. It would just lead to more questions about why she didn't want to.

"So," he continued, "just try to talk to me and see what happens."

"Maybe what happens is I fuck you up forever."

He smiled. "You're adorable when you swear."

"It's not funny, Jed."

He stopped and grabbed both of her hands in his.

"Look, you need allies. I might be the lamest one ever, but I think this is worth trying. What if you can make your own army of Dreamwalkers?"

"One person is not an army."

"No. But it is at least company." He smiled. "And what if I double your chance of success?"

Finn felt herself tearing up. She looked away, but he grabbed her chin and brought it back so he could look her in the eye.

"What if you get hurt?" she asked.

"Get hurt? No way. I have the kick-assiest bodyguard in Dreamland."

She knew that Jed really wanted to help her, and it was possible he could. Only Finn didn't want to worry about anyone else. She knew she should just tell him no and get home before she changed her mind.

She kissed him instead.

*　*　*

Jed insisted on walking her home . . .

Then up to the door . . .

And into the house.

Nana smiled when they walked in, then she invited Jed to stay for dinner.

TWENTY

Her mother was already at the table. She stood up and hugged Jed. "You are much taller than I remember," she told him.

"I come from a tall people," he said adorably.

Jed pulled out Nana's chair for her. Nana looked at him, at Finn, and then she sat down. She smiled into her plate but didn't say anything. Finn sat down quickly so he wouldn't try to help her with her chair. Nana had enough material already.

They made small talk while they passed the food around the table. How were Jed's parents? Did his grandmother's hip replacement turn out okay? What was he going to do with his summer? Jed answered while spooning heaping mounds of food onto his plate. He asked Julia about life in Norway, Nana about her herb garden and how she got things to grow year-round. It was only when Jed was serving himself a second helping of pot roast that the conversation lagged. The room was silent, except for the tapping of the serving spoon as Jed tried to knock a stuck potato onto his plate. When it finally slid off, he looked up and saw Julia and Nana watching him.

"I know," he said quietly.

They remained silent.

"I know everything. Or most of it, I think. I've thought about it a lot, and I just want you to know . . ." He bit his lip in a way Finn had never seen before. She realized that Nervous Jed was not a Jed she knew. He set the serving spoon back into the pot roast before he continued. "I just want you to know that she's going to be fine. Finn is the smartest, most capable, amazing person I've ever met, and she's going to be fine." And with that, Jed stabbed a bite from his plate and shoved it into his mouth.

Finn turned to her mom. Julia was looking down at her plate. Finn suspected she was trying not to cry. Nana, on the other hand, was looking right at her granddaughter.

"Yes," Nana said. "Yes, she is."

TWENTY-ONE

Finn walked Jed to the door after dinner, and he made her promise that she would try to come get him from his dream. Finn resisted, but Jed wouldn't let her close the door until she said yes. When she did, he gave her a quick kiss on the lips and then headed into the cold. She heard the crunch of his feet even after he'd turned the corner and disappeared.

The cold air felt good, and Finn took longer than she should have to close the door. She heard her mother walk into the den behind her.

"There's a breeze blowing through the kitchen."

Finn closed the door and turned around.

"I've always liked him," her mother said before heading back the way she came.

Jed had been gone for hours, but Finn was still wide awake, sitting against the headboard of her bed rather than lying down. She hadn't even tried to do her homework. She knew that she'd just stare at whatever was in front of her, moving her pencil around in some doodle shape, wondering why she wasn't tired yet.

She'd heard her mother and Nana go to bed a while ago. She didn't know if they were asleep, but the house was quiet, so she assumed they were. Or maybe they were just lying in the dark, staring at nothing, like she was.

Saying good night to them had been weird. Everyone had something to say, but nobody said it. Still, Finn had decided that caring too much was better than caring too little, and she thought the weirdness was a sign of the former, rather than the latter.

She wanted to be asleep, rather than wishing she was asleep. She'd counted sheep, counted backward from a thousand, multiplied fractions in her head. Nothing worked. She couldn't ask Nana for any of the weird tea. That might put her too asleep. But she had no idea how to overcome the nervousness she felt.

She spun around on the bed and put her feet on the floor. On her nightstand was a crumpled piece of paper. It had Rafe's phone number written on it. He'd given it to her the other day. She grabbed her phone and dialed the number. He'd probably be asleep, but what the hell? Why should he sleep, if she couldn't?

He answered after two rings. "Hello."

"It's Finn."

"It's late."

"I can't sleep."

"Guilty conscience?"

"Nerves, I think."

"What do you have to be nervous about?"

Finn didn't answer. She didn't trust Rafe, but she wasn't sure why anymore. She thought he was probably a good guy.

"I think I know how to help Noah."

She heard rustling and assumed he'd sat up in bed.

"What?"

"I'm not sure, exactly, what happened to him, but I feel like I know how to find him." She didn't say out loud the "sort of" she felt.

Rafe exhaled. "This is way beyond you, Finn. Tell me what you know. I'll find someone who can do what needs to be done."

"No. It's got to be me. Only . . . now I can't fall asleep."

He laughed.

"It's not funny," she said.

"No, it's ironic. Which is different."

"I know what irony is."

"You know what irony is in a book. You don't know what irony is in life. You're way too young."

"How do I go to sleep?"

"You don't."

"What the hell does that mean?"

"I'm not going to say I think you should, but you know how to get to the River without being asleep."

He was right. She just had been too balled up in herself to think of it.

"Right."

"And Finn?"

"Yeah."

"'Ponder and deliberate before you make a move,'" he said. "That's from *The Art of War*."

"I've been pondering a long time. I'm glad to have a chance to finally do something." She started to hang up and then stopped herself. "Rafe?"

"Yeah?"

"Thanks."

"You're welcome. I'll talk to you tomorrow."

Never had the phrase "talk to you tomorrow" seemed so loaded.

She set her phone on the bedside table and closed her eyes. She focused on the darkness in front of her eyelids, breathed in and out.

She saw a glimmer and felt a rush of air, as though she was being sucked into something.

Something big.

Was she ready?

TWENTY-TWO

Finn ignored the screams coming from the River. Tonight she couldn't help anyone but Noah. She'd spent the day thinking about last night's dream; she was sure Noah had walked into it to come see her. Why do that if he didn't have something to say? She'd woken up before the dream ended. She felt sure that going back to it would give her something useful, maybe even the secret that Noah had been chasing.

Finn reached her right hand back toward her shoulder. A sword appeared, strapped to her back. The black blade hissed as Finn pulled it from its sheath. Finn looked downstream. Just like last night, the dreams in the distance were less vivid, except for a few bright spots, which were farther away than before. She reached for the closest one. Noah had something to tell her. She knew he did.

Her arm stretched thin, pulling the rest of her into a thread of Finn-ness and—

She was back in her room, her dream self still floating above the bed. Finn stood where she was, waiting. She knew that Noah would come, and then, he did. Or more like appeared. Her back had been to the door last night, and she hadn't noticed how he materialized out of nowhere.

"I don't want to wake you, Finn."

Noah was looking at the sleeping Finn hovering above the bed; he still had his green Lochran and sword. Finn concentrated on her breathing, trying to keep calm so she wouldn't freak out and break the dream apart.

Noah walked to the bed and sat down.

"There are so many things I want to tell you," he said. He reached to put a hand on the sleeping Finn but stopped himself. "But . . . I don't think I should. You'll just worry."

He looked so small. How had she not noticed he'd lost weight?

"I've seen so many amazing things. It's been like a video game on steroids. Except I'm the game. And the player. And when you lose, the stakes are so high."

He sighed. Finn could tell he was tired. "There are so many people who need help," he told her sleeping self. "It's . . . overwhelming. I know I can't help everyone. There's no way I could help everyone." As he talked, Finn carefully walked around the room so she could get a better look at his face. She wondered if she looked as tired as Noah did. Was the disadvantage of being a Dreamwalker that you didn't get enough sleep? That must be the very definition of irony, no matter if it were book irony or life irony.

"Jed likes you, by the way," Noah threw out. "I'm not going to tell you how I know that. 'Cause it'll be embarrassing for both of us."

Finn felt herself blush. Thank God he didn't go on. Listening to her brother talk about Jed's sex dreams might be more than she could handle.

"I hate keeping secrets from you, Finn. I know you'd understand how I feel. If nothing else, you'd make sure I didn't do anything stupid. Or you'd tell me I was doing something stupid and bribe me to stop by making cookies or something." He smiled. "It wouldn't work, but I love your cookies." Finn could see the sadness in him, a slight droop in his shoulders.

Come on, Noah, she thought, tell me what's on your mind.

He was quiet a long time and then whispered, "Do you ever think about Dad?"

What?

Of course she did. A lot more recently, since the dream where she was trapped in the room. But even before that. She realized that she and Noah didn't really talk about their father. They hadn't in a long time.

"I wonder," Noah continued, "if maybe—"

Finn smelled sulfur right before the room EXPLODED. She turned and saw the man with the buffalo mask charge toward Noah. In the shadows behind him, something fled into the darkness of the hallway.

The man swung his weapon: a stick about four feet long with dragonlike skulls on each end and covered with glowing spikes.

As the stick arced through the air, it seemed to groan, and the sound caused the floating Dream Finn to stir.

Noah raised his sword to defend himself. The creature's stick crashed down on Noah's sword and—

Everything froze.

The room became completely silent.

What the hell?

Finn stepped forward, but nothing else moved. Noah and the man were midbattle. Dream Finn was frozen, too, her eyes now open, her face contorted in fear. What had happened? Rafe had never mentioned anything like this, neither had Sydney Norwich. The only thing that made sense to her was that in real life she woke up. This was the end of the dream. Noah and the man had probably been expelled from the dream, back into the River.

Finn approached Noah. He didn't look small anymore. He looked fierce. The muscles in his arms were taut as he protected himself. Whatever was happening at this moment had not surprised him.

Finn circled the man in the buffalo mask. A sense of dread and decay clung to him. His skin was the palest white she'd ever seen. The burning sores all over it oozed a dark pus-like substance. The animal hides that clung to the lower half of his body were covered in crimson patches. Finn couldn't help but think they were dried blood. His weapon, gripped tightly in his hands, was smooth, as if he'd been holding it, wielding it, for a long time. Up close, it was easy to see that the glowing spikes were Lochrans. She reached out and touched one. Even in this already-dreamed dream, she could feel its power.

Finn stepped forward, angry. This man was attacking her brother. Somehow, she wasn't sure how yet, he was responsible for Noah's coma.

She grabbed the mask to rip it off his head, so she could see his face, and only when she touched it did she realize that it wasn't a mask at all. It was the cleaned-out head of a buffalo. She yanked on it, but, like the book she'd tried to pick up before, it wouldn't budge. This already-dreamed dream could not be changed.

Finn leaned in, looked at his eyes. The pupils were indistinct from the irises around them, and the blackness was disconcerting. Even frozen, the man's fury was unmistakable.

Finn turned to look at her brother. He was frozen. What was the harm in touching him? She put a hand on his cheek.

"What have you gotten yourself into, Noah?"

She waited. As she always did. To see if he would answer. But like every moment for the last nine months, there was silence.

"Okay, I get it. Still with the secrets. I'll figure it out," she whispered into the silence.

She took one last look at the man in the buffalo head. Was this Jed's bad guy, builder of armies? If so, Jed might be right that she needed help. It might be too big for her to handle alone. And so she reached out her hand and found herself—

Back in the River. She looked upstream toward the crush of images that flowed her way.

"Jed," she said quietly, praying she wouldn't interrupt anything embarrassing, and she was instantly relieved to be standing in a desert, sand as far as the eye could see. Squatting nearby was Jed, alone, hunched over something on the ground. Finn approached him. As she got closer, she saw he'd used his finger to draw something in the sand. The maze. Sydney's maze. Noah's maze. An army of ants moved inside it. Jed was watching them intently. Because there was no way out, the ants just moved back and forth in the trenches he'd *created, creating blobs of ants when they reached the end of a blocked passageway.*

After a moment, Jed reached over and created a new opening in a side wall so that they could escape. The ants flowed out and began to march away, one after another. It took only a few moments for the maze to clear.

"Hi, Jed."

He looked up. "Hi, Finn."

"How's it going?"

"Pretty good."

"What are you doing out here?"

"It's peaceful."

"It is. Do you remember what we talked about?"

"Raisins?"

"No."

"Then, no. I don't."

"You wanted to help me find Noah."

"That's a great idea."

"Should we give it a go?"

She reached out a hand, and Jed took it. "Absolutely." As he stood, his legs unfolded. He seemed taller in the dream.

"Hold on, okay. Don't let go," Finn told him. "We're going to try something."

"Okay."

Finn looked at Jed. He was smiling. At her. She squeezed his hand, then closed her eyes. She heard the River of Dreams. Jed was still holding her hand. When she opened her eyes, he was looking around. "Holy—"

And then he was gone, her hand empty.

Finn started to panic. She told herself to wake up and then remembered she hadn't gone to sleep. She looked around, saw a gauzy spot in the images, and floated toward it. She pushed through and—

Was back in her room, on her bed. Her cell phone was buzzing. She picked it up. Jed had texted her.

Wuz that U?

U tell me, she typed back.

Desert and . . . what the hell . . . He followed it with a series of emojis: a wave followed by a bolt of lightning, a music note, and clashing cymbals. She was thinking about how to respond when he sent her a poo emoji.

What's that mean? she wrote back.

That shit was real, Finn. That shit was real. He followed this with a smiley face.

TWENTY-THREE

Finn lay awake a long time before she realized she wasn't going to be able to rest. She went to the kitchen to get some water and heard Eddie scratching at the carpet in Noah's room to make a comfortable nest for himself. She walked in, and Eddie stopped. He looked up at her a beat before flopping to the floor.

Finn went and sat next to Noah.

A thin shaft of moonlight peeked through the curtain and fell across his face, almost like it had been painted on. Finn traced it along her brother's cheek. She wished he'd told her about being a Dreamwalker. She wished he had asked for help with whatever, or whoever, was troubling him. Finn was afraid that maybe he did, maybe he gave her a thousand little clues that something was going on and she was too caught up in her own high school nothingness to see them. She hoped that wasn't true.

In the months he'd been in a coma, she'd relived so many of the important moments of their lives. In an article on neuroscience she'd read soon after he'd gone into his coma, she'd learned the very act of remembering something changed it. The emotions you brought to the memory reshaped it in ways that you couldn't even know. After she'd read the article, Finn had tried hard not to think about the past when she was depressed or upset, because she didn't want all her memories of him to be painted with a melancholy brush. Of all the people she'd ever met, he laughed the easiest. Big laughs, small laughs, some that never seemed to escape this own head.

She hoped wherever he was, his own memories weren't being altered. She hoped fear didn't cause all the good things he'd known to slip away. She hoped he at least had his memories to hold on to.

She was wide awake. There was no point in trying to sleep. So Finn sat there for hours and reminded Noah of the places they'd been, the people they'd met, the things they'd done. She told him his favorite joke and, using only that strip of moonlight, read him a chapter from his favorite book.

Finn remembered.

For both of them.

TWENTY-FOUR

Noah felt a breeze stir. He didn't know where it came from. He looked around, wondering if the monster was near. He held his breath, hoping it wasn't.

In the silence, he heard something. A voice, soothing. Almost like a melody from a favorite song.

He was so tired, and his chest . . . it hurt. He fought to keep his eyes open. He had been fighting against sleep for so long, afraid if he gave in, the spiders would crawl down and build their webs on top of him, or that the creature himself would return and finally kill him.

He wanted to go home. For so long, he prayed that someone would come save him.

Something about the voice was so familiar. And, finally, he remembered.

"Finn."

He whispered quietly so the monster would not awaken.

TWENTY-FIVE

Mom and Nana took good long looks at her at breakfast but said nothing other than good morning, as if acting normal would make everything normal. Finn didn't volunteer any details about her evening. She just ate a good breakfast. They couldn't worry too much as long as she was eating, right?

Jed didn't wait for her to get to him. He was waiting at the end of her corner and screamed "Unbelievable!" as soon as he saw her. She didn't reply, just walked toward him as he sprinted toward her, talking all the way. "That was amazing. I mean, it only lasted for about a second, so I couldn't get a good look around, but still, Finn . . . unbelievable."

When he reached her, he grabbed her backpack and her hand. Words spilled out of him in a nonstop stream. One incomplete thought after another.

"Loud. I can't believe how loud it was . . . And so many . . . How do you track them? . . . Or is that not the point . . . I think

I saw a dinosaur . . . Maybe an alligator . . . It's a dream, no reason it can't be a dinosaur . . . I didn't expect them to move so fast and flow like that . . . I know you said 'river.' In retrospect, not sure what I thought you meant by that. 'River' is a pretty clear image. It was just bigger than any river I've ever seen . . ."

He went on like that almost the whole way to school, which was fine. Finn was only half listening. She was thinking, as she had most of the night, about the man in the buffalo head. He was like a Dreamwalker, though clearly an evil one. And all those Lochrans. Why did he have so many?

Finn realized it was quiet. Jed had stopped talking. They were walking, but he was just looking at her. "Normally you're my favorite conversation partner. Today, not so much."

"I was thinking about some things."

"No problem. I wasn't really talking about anything important. Just the most mind-blowing experience this side of LSD."

"You've done LSD?"

"No, but I've read books. Anything you want to tell me?"

"Isn't your mind blown enough for one day?"

"Depends." He dropped her hand and threw his arm around her shoulders. "You looked totally hot in your Dreamwalker gear."

"I was wearing sweatpants."

"And a sword."

"Ah. The sword." She'd forgotten about it.

"Can I get a sword?"

"I don't know."

"Well, if I get a vote, I'd like a sword. I'll be quiet now."

He pulled her close, and they walked in silence the rest of the way to school.

TWENTY-SIX

The best thing, maybe the only good thing, about Mr. Newsome was he didn't really care about actual classroom attendance. If you wanted to go to the library and do research on Guy Fawkes and the Gunpowder Plot, a fascinating bit of treason they'd never actually studied in class because it was way too interesting, then you could ask to go to the library. When you came back to class, either that hour or the next day, Mr. Newsome simply wanted you to share something you'd learned. Wikipedia was usually the source, but the tidbits were almost always interesting, perfect for dinnertime, and allowed parents to feel their tax dollars weren't being wasted. Finn rarely took advantage of the privilege to leave, but today, the library was where she needed to be.

She told Mr. Newsome that, while she was researching her term paper, she'd read that James I's heart had been taken on a pilgrimage to the Holy Land. She wanted to know if it was true. Mr. Newsome sent her off with a hall pass and an admonition to keep it PG-13. He didn't want to hear about "bloody entrails." She didn't bother to point out that entrails were digestively related and had nothing to do with the heart. She simply said "Of course" and went on her way.

Getting to the library meant Finn had to walk by the main administrative hallway. She glanced down the corridor and was surprised to see Marcus sitting on the bench outside the main office with Deborah, who was crying.

Finn was about to stop and head toward them, to see if she could help, when Mrs. Olsen, a guidance counselor and by far the best adult in the school, came out of the office. Finn kept moving, stopping to look back only when she'd cleared the hallway. Mrs. Olsen sat next to Deborah and spoke to her. Deborah kept crying, but after a moment, she nodded. Mrs. Olsen stood up, keeping a hand on Deborah's arm as she stood up, too. They headed toward the office with Marcus trailing behind them. Only then did Finn notice another woman standing inside the room. Finn didn't recognize her, but when she turned sideways so everyone could walk by her into the office, Finn saw the flash of a badge.

And a gun.

The woman was a detective, a police detective.

Deborah or Marcus, maybe Mrs. Olsen. Someone had called the police.

Finn watched the office door close.

She leaned back against the wall, out of sight. Deborah was

going to get help. She was going to get away from the parents who were abusing her. It didn't mean her problems were over, but hopefully it meant they couldn't hurt her anymore.

There was no way to know if Finn had helped make it happen, but . . . maybe. A little. Maybe her walk into Marcus's subconscious had gotten him to help Deborah. Finn could barely breathe.

She felt . . . what? Grateful? Relieved? No, those weren't quite right.

Surprised. She felt surprised. Even though she had wanted this outcome, had tried to help facilitate this outcome, she was surprised it had actually happened.

Correlation isn't causality, Jed liked to say.

Screw that.

The surprise faded away, and gratitude and relief flowed in to take its place. Deborah was going to get some help.

She heard footsteps in the hallway. If a teacher caught her loitering, she'd be sent back to Mr. Newsome's class. So she pushed herself off the wall and continued on to the library.

She managed to find an open computer in the back of the library, where nobody liked to sit because the sun shone directly through the window and made it hot even on cold days. She peeled off her sweater and was still uncomfortably warm. She was certain that nobody else would put up with the heat and that she'd be able to work in peace.

She quickly looked up the facts about King James's heart.

A doctoral thesis by a woman at Edinburgh offered a smidgen of proof that it made a round trip to the Holy Land before being returned to his body by a knight from the Order of Saint John. The part she thought Mr. Newsome would like is that the Order of Saint John eventually turned into the Military Order of Malta, which still has sovereignty under international law and can issue its own passports.

That bit of housekeeping finished, Finn turned to why she'd really come. She needed to know more about the man in the buffalo head, though she had no idea where to start. She typed "buffalo" into a search engine, which got her a lot of articles about animals and football teams. She moved on to "buffalo" and "ritual," which led to a list of Native American ceremonies and a couple of stories about the near-extinction of the animal in the late nineteenth century. In one of the articles, she saw a drawing from 1851 of a man wearing a buffalo head as part of a dance. She typed "buffalo head" and "ritual" and found hundreds of images of people wearing real buffalo heads. None of them were right, either. Perhaps the animal she was looking for might be buffalo adjacent. She was about to move on when . . .

There he was.

A drawing by a man named Henri Breuil of a creature standing on its two legs, but with the head of a horned animal.

The drawing didn't look like a buffalo, and it also didn't look like the photo of the fifteen-thousand-year-old French cave painting it was based on. What it did look like—the shape of the horns, the stare—was the man she'd seen last night.

Scholars had given a name to the cave painting. They called him "The Sorcerer."

Somewhere deep inside, a feeling bubbled up. She knew this was important. She knew that she was closer to figuring out what had happened to Noah than ever before. She wasn't at the finish line. But she was finally in the race.

TWENTY-SEVEN

Finn showed Jed the image of the sorcerer from the cave. "The Shadow," he said. She knew there was more, so she waited. "From the Hero's Journey. Gollum. Voldemort . . . the Sorcerer."

"The bad guy."

"Yes, except a bad guy never thinks they're the bad guy. They think the good guy is the bad guy, because the hero is trying to stop them from controlling the world and creating order, their kind of order, out of chaos."

"So this sorcerer is trying to control the dream world?"

"If that River isn't the definition of chaos, I don't know what is."

Jed was a big fan of the villain. In his mind, they didn't get enough credit. Without Darth Vader, he'd once told her, *Star Wars* was just a boring movie about a cynical pilot and Bigfoot. Because without Vader, there's no Luke, no Leia, and no personification of the darker aspects of the Force.

"You said he had 'flaming sores'?" Jed asked.

"Yep."

"It's the darkness within oozing out."

"There was a lot of oozing. And . . . his weapon. It was a stick covered in Lochrans. A bunch of Lochrans."

Jed looked at the printout of the Sorcerer. "How old did you say this cave painting was?"

"Fifteen thousand years."

"What if he's one of the first Dreamwalkers, or *the* first? He's on that wall because people knew he had magic. He cured them of the terrors that came in the night."

"Say I buy it. He'd be fifteen thousand years old now," Finn pointed out.

"Very dead."

They walked in silence for a half block. Then Finn stopped. Jed took a step or two before he realized she wasn't next to him. He turned around.

"You were right before," Finn told him. "About the philosopher's stone. This guy is dead in our world. But he's alive in the dream world . . . because of the Lochrans. What if the glowing spikes are Lochrans he's stolen from other Dreamwalkers because he needs their energy to stay alive?"

"The hero must die for him to be immortal."

"Noah's not dead!" she snapped, startling Jed and causing him to take an involuntary step away from her. But it took him only a second to recover.

"Of course not, Finn. I know that. I'm sorry. That wasn't what I meant." He bent his head toward her forehead. "I'm really sorry."

A tear slid down Finn's cheek. The wet trail stiffened as it froze against her skin. She concentrated on the warmth of Jed's head on hers until she was finally calm. "Noah doesn't have his Lochran. The Sorcerer laid a trap, and Noah fell into it. That's why he can't get home."

Jed kissed her gently on the forehead. "Which is why we are going to go get him."

TWENTY-EIGHT

Finn had been thinking about her plan for days. Well, not so much "thinking about," more realizing that she didn't have a lot of good ideas about how to proceed. She kept hoping for a flash of inspiration, and all she got were small flickers of the obvious. Tonight, having come up with nothing new, she was relieved when Nana called down the hall to say dinner was ready.

When Finn came into the kitchen, she saw her mother in with Noah. Julia was checking a bag on his IV stand. It was a new one: small, filled with a clear liquid.

"What's the IV for?"

"The nurse came by today." Nana paused, as though she was weighing what to say, or whether to say it. After a beat, she continued. "She listened to his lungs, thought he had a bronchial infection."

"At the hospital, they said that could lead to pneumonia."

"Yes, but you and I, we got onto it very quickly. The doctor ordered antibiotics. I think . . . it'll be fine."

Finn knew Nana wanted her not to worry about it. But how could she not? It was clear that Noah was getting sicker every day. She slid into her seat. Nana pulled a casserole dish out of the oven. Cheese bubbled on the top of it. Lasagna. "I made your favorite," she said with a smile.

"Lasagna's not my favorite."

"I meant chocolate cake with cream-cheese icing." She gestured with her head to a platter on the counter. The cake was beautiful: three layers, a thick wave of frosting rippling across the top of it.

"How are the three of us going to eat that giant cake?"

Nana set the lasagna in the middle of the table. "Jed can have some."

"He's allergic to chocolate."

"Didn't know that." Nana sat down. "Then I'll just have to freeze a few pieces for your brother." She put a hand on Finn's arm and squeezed it. "Would that be okay?"

Finn smiled. "That'd be great."

Finn ate two pieces of cake. Not huge pieces, but two pieces nonetheless. It was delicious. When she'd eaten as many crumbs as she could pick up with her fork, she stood and carried her plate to the dishwasher.

Her mom stopped her. "I'll do the dishes, Finn."

Finn put her plate on the counter and turned around. She leaned back. She was really full. And oddly content.

"What'd you put in the cake, Nana?"

"Are you accusing me of spiking it?"

"I'm wondering."

"Love." Her mother smiled.

"Lemon bacopa, which actually tastes more like lime," Nana added when Finn didn't move. "And love."

"Lime-flavored lemon bacopa. What's it do?"

"Balances the heaviness of the chocolate." Finn raised an eyebrow. "And it's good for focus."

Finn looked between the two of them and smiled. As hard as all this was for her, it must be so much worse for them. At least she got to do something. All Nana could do was add lime-flavored herbs to cakes. Her mom could do even less.

"Remember your pages from the monastery, Mom?"

Julia nodded.

"I think . . ." Her mom and Nana both leaned forward. "I think *Malum* is important. There is something dark and old at the root of all this." Her mom opened her mouth to speak, and Finn rushed into the silence. "The good news is I've seen it, and I think I know what it wants. And, even though he's got home-field advantage, he's alone. I'm not. I have you guys, and I have lemon bacopa."

Telling them about Jed would raise too many questions, she'd decided, including one she'd already asked herself, like how she could let him get involved in something so dangerous. And, worse, her mom might want to come with Finn, too. When Finn said no—because she would definitely say no—there'd be a fight. Better to skip that and give them fewer things to object to.

She thought they might still try to stop her. It was, after all, their job to protect her, make sure she got to adulthood safely. It was what they had been doing since the day she was born. She'd seen the pictures from the hospital. Her mom and dad tired and beaming, holding her close to their hearts. Nana kissing her forehead, the only part of Finn not wrapped in blankets or covered in a knit cap. She was theirs to love and protect. They had wiped her tears and her butt, knowing that the day would come when Finn would go off on her own and make her way in the world. They wanted her to be ready. They did everything they could to get her ready.

They just hadn't known that that day would come so soon.

Finn waited, prepared to let them say whatever they needed to say, but they stood, silent, for the longest time. The only sound was Eddie breathing loudly in Noah's room.

Finally, Finn's mom crossed to Finn and wrapped her arms around her. She pulled Finn as tight as she could. She was holding on so tight it hurt a little. And then, she let go and leaned back and looked Finn in the eye.

"There is nothing you can't do, Finn," her mom said. "You have spent too much of your life hiding your light, but anyone who was really looking could see it. Now maybe . . . you do, too." Her mom let go of her shoulders, and Finn realized Nana was standing next to them. She was holding a small plate with another piece of cake on it.

"In case you get hungry," she said. Finn took the plate, and Nana stood on tiptoe to kiss Finn on the cheek.

Nana smiled. Finn took her cake and headed down the hall to her room.

When Finn picked up her phone, there were ten messages from Jed, all with attachments or links to the Internet. All of it was about the Sorcerer, shamans in general, or about shamans gone wrong. He had highlighted an article about how shamans do what they do and triple-underlined a passage about how the forces of good will never let a shaman do bad. It was practically an honors-thesis amount of research.

You know, Finn typed, *if you put this much work into school . . .*

She had barely pushed Send when his reply appeared. *Get an A in third-year Spanish = save the world? I don't think so.* And then a moment later, *C U later. xo.*

Finn stared at the "xo." They'd typed that a thousand times at the end of texts. It started as a joke, after Jed had wondered aloud if the size of the letters indicated some variation in the amount of affection. Small hugs and kisses. Sometimes, one of them would type a hundred of them, with one capitalized in the middle. Sometimes just an *x*, sometimes just an *o*. Jed went through a phase where he tried to send Morse code messages using the *x*'s and *o*'s as dots and dashes, but when he realized Finn wasn't going to learn Morse code just to know what he was saying, he stopped.

It was always a joke.

Or so she thought. But now . . .

C U soon. xo, she typed. It wasn't too few if you meant it.

TWENTY-NINE

Finn got into bed fully dressed. If the Sorcerer surprised her when she arrived in the River, she didn't want to be wearing pajama bottoms and a tank top. She'd also tucked the printout of the cave painting into her jeans pocket, but as she waited for sleep to come, her mind kept spinning. What else did she need? It was like packing for a trip when you didn't know where you were going and were pretty sure your bags weren't going to arrive even if you did.

She sat up and opened the drawer of her nightstand. It was mostly full of crap: pencils, scraps of paper, change from her pocket. But there were a few useful items. She pulled out the headlamp Nana had put in for emergencies. Jed wouldn't be able to create his own light, but maybe this would work for him. She grabbed her Swiss Army knife so she could give him that, too. She felt more prepared with just those two things, so she started to close the drawer. She heard something rattle against the side. She pulled it open again and saw the rosary that Sharon Lewis, a classmate, had given her, resting on top of her favorite picture of her and Noah.

They were young, dressed like cowboys. Or at least he was. He'd gotten a Woody costume for his birthday. Finn was wearing a baseball cap and had a dish towel wrapped around her waist, a gun-shaped stick tucked into it. If the size of their smiles were any indication, though, neither of them cared about the lameness of her costume.

And it hadn't gotten in the way of their mission: "Making the world safe for small birds and rodents," her mom said. Because all they did was run around the neighborhood, saving birds and squirrels from Herman, a neighbor's cat.

Finn grabbed the picture and put it in her breast pocket. When she turned back to close the drawer, Saint Patrick was staring at her.

She remembered when she'd gotten the rosary. Sharon— who might be the shiest person at school—had walked up to her in the cafeteria a couple of weeks after Noah went into the coma and handed it over with a quick "I'll be praying for you." Finn had been so surprised she'd forgotten to say thank you. But it had been one of those acts of kindness that had moved Finn during those dark days. She'd looped the rosary through a strap on her backpack and carried it around for a couple of weeks, until she started to feel like people were staring at it and wondering if she'd undergone some kind of religious conversion to save her brother. No one ever said anything, but she felt judged. Normally, Finn didn't care what people thought. But with the rosary, for some reason, she had. She'd removed it from her bag and thrown it inside the drawer, and she hadn't thought about it since.

She picked up the rosary and wrapped it around her wrist. Saint Patrick. Former slave, not even Irish, never canonized so he wasn't really a saint.

Give me all you've got, Saint Pat. Give me all you've got.

Finn lay down on top of the covers and closed her eyes.

The River crashed into her harder than it ever had before: an explosion of sights, sounds, and emotions that almost knocked her off her feet. It was like standing at the edge of the beach when a hurricane approached, or at least the way it looked on the news, since Finn had never been to the beach or seen a hurricane up close.

She steadied herself. Why was the River more out of control than usual?

Finn reached out and grabbed a dream and found herself—

At the airport. Travelers scurried back and forth, moving quickly toward their gates. Except for . . .

One man on the moving sidewalk. He was walking the wrong way, pulling a suitcase that was as big as he was. Late for your plane: an ordinary anxiety dream. Except . . . there was something else. Finn stood still. What was it? A sound. Finn filtered out the sounds of the travelers and the announcements and was left with . . .

A buzzing. No. More a crackling, like an electrical short. She could hear it and, weirdly, feel it. She raised her arm. The hairs on it stood up, like they were full of static electricity.

She looked at the man on the moving sidewalk. His belongings were bursting from the suitcase and wrapping around his legs, slowing him down even more. He looked more than anxious. He looked terrified.

Finn stepped out of the dream and—

Back to the River. She grabbed another dream and was—

High above the ground in a cloudless sky. The sun blazed overhead. Finn hovered and listened. She felt more than heard the sound here, too. She looked around for the source and saw a woman flying toward her. No, plummeting toward her. The woman's hands were pressed against her ears. She was losing altitude, but when she tried to extend her arms to fly, her face contorted in pain. She rushed to put her hands back over her ears. The anxious buzzing was too much.

Finn zoomed over and grabbed her. The woman looked shocked, scared. Finn held her for a moment and then conjured a giant eagle that flew in and gently grabbed the woman by the back of her shirt. Finn watched the woman and the eagle fly away, and then they disappeared as Finn found herself—

Back in the River.

She reached for another dream. The same buzzing vibration. She threw it back, grabbed another and another and another. It was there in all of them. Fear, vibrating through the River. She could feel it coursing through her. Her heart pounding.

She closed her eyes and took a deep breath, then another. She concentrated on the rising and falling of her chest. She felt the

Lochran grow warm against her skin. The buzzing faded. She felt better. Time to go.

She focused on the blackness in front of her eyes and thought about . . . Jed.

The lights were off, but she could see him sitting at a desk, rocking back and forth, tapping a pencil on a piece of paper in front of him. He was saying something, but she couldn't hear what it was. Finn stepped closer.

"Hi, Jed."

He ignored her, just kept rocking and saying, "No, no, no." His dream was full of anxiety, too.

She rested a hand on his shoulder. "It's okay, Jed. I can help." She pulled the headlamp out of her pocket and pushed the power button. The room filled with light. Finn didn't have any idea whether it worked because that's what lamps do or because she had the power to turn it on, but it didn't matter. She was grateful for the brightness it brought to the room.

"No, no, no."

Finn put the headlamp around his head, holding it in place while she concentrated on filling the room with silence. After a moment, he stopped rocking and stopped mumbling. She tried again. "Hi, Jed."

"Hey, Finn." He reached up and touched the headlamp, like he'd just realized it was there. She rested a hand on his.

"I'd leave it there. I think it'll make our trip easier."

"It's cold in here, isn't it?"

"It is a little cold."

He reached and touched the Lochran around her neck, and she had a sudden vision of the Sorcerer reaching for it. Without thinking, she pulled away.

"Sorry," he said.

"It's okay. I just didn't expect it. But you've given me an idea." She reached for the Lochran. Rafe told her he'd ripped his off. The Sorcerer wanted hers. He had a bunch of them. Obviously, it wasn't permanently stuck around her neck. She wondered . . . Finn put her hands on the Lochran and pulled, gently. It got a little bit larger, so she pulled a little bit more and then more, until it was big enough to wiggle it over her shoulders and down to her hips. Then she pinched it to make it smaller before she pulled her shirt over it.

"I can still see it," Jed told her.

"Yes, but maybe it'll be harder to grab with my T-shirt and jacket in the way. How much do you remember, Jed?"

"About what?"

"About what we are trying to do?"

He looked at her, puzzled.

"You want to help me save Noah."

"Of course I do."

"That was stupid. Of course you do. I guess I'm just wondering how much you remembered about what we are trying to do." She reached into her pocket and pulled out the Swiss Army knife. She gave it to him. "Don't hurt yourself."

"You say that like I'll hurt myself." He smiled. "Which is smart." He reached over and brushed some hair away from her eyes. "The maze. The bird. Sydney. Guy with the antlers. Good. Evil. Best girl-friend ever."

She smiled. It had taken only a few minutes. Dream Jed was like real Jed.

She closed her eyes and took a deep breath. She heard Jed take a sudden step back. "Holy crap," he said. She opened her eyes. He was staring at her in disbelief and then reached out and touched the sword that now existed in a sheath on her back. "Your knife is better than my knife."

"I think we can agree that if you had a bigger knife, you'd only hurt yourself worse."

"True that, but still . . ."

She took his hand. "Ready?"

"Where are we going, Finn?"

"To find a hummingbird that will lead us into a trap."

"Is that a good idea?"

"I hope so. Close your eyes."

He did. And then Finn closed hers and—

She heard the whirring of the hummingbird. It was very close, and she could tell it was swooping, up and down, the way hummingbirds do when they are trying to attract a mate or intimidate a rival.

She opened her eyes. Jed was already watching the bird, the light from his headlamp tracking it, occasionally flashing off its iridescent feathers.

Finn looked around. They were in a flat, rocky area. Not at all the kind of place she would expect a hummingbird. But this one looked just like the hummingbird she'd seen in that first dream of Noah, where the two of them were floating below the ice.

Now the bird was just flying, up and down, in a giant U-shape, making a show for her.

She put out her arm, one finger extended. The hummingbird flew over and landed.

"Well," Jed observed, "that's not something you see every day."

"I think this is our guide."

"Do you trust it?"

"My brother's in a coma. So no."

"Exactly what I was thinking. So what do we do?"

"Follow it until following seems dumb." Finn lifted the hummingbird until they were eye to eye. "Lead on, little guy. And, while I find you very beautiful, I will crush you like a bug if I have to."

The hummingbird lifted off from Finn's finger and headed away.

"Did that bird smile at you?" Jed asked incredulously.

"That won't be the strangest thing we see, if it did."

Finn followed the bird. She knew Jed was behind her because the light of his lamp created a shadow of her legs against the ground. The shadow stretched out ten feet in front of her.

She was a giant.

THIRTY

For some reason, Noah was thinking about cowboys.

Actually, he was thinking about Woody from Toy Story. A long time ago, he'd had a costume. He pretended to be a sheriff while he chased the neighbor's cat.

What was the cat's name?

Herbert . . . No. Herman. Big and gray, his tail white, which made him easier to find, even when he hid in the bushes.

Herman liked to catch birds and mice. He'd parade up and down the street. Showing off. Noah thought Herman was a bully. He cried once when he saw Herman out in front of the house with a baby robin in his mouth.

Finn thought if they made enough noise, the other creatures would get scared off so Herman couldn't get them. They ran up and down the street for hours, clanking pans and shouting, until Herman would finally slink through the cat door into his house. Sometimes, Noah felt sorry for the cat, and he'd give him a can of tuna to make up for the animal snacks he was missing.

Sheriff Noah and Sheriff Finn.

It was a good memory. Noah let it settle into the dark places in the back of his mind, almost like a light in a dark room.

THIRTY-ONE

They'd been walking a long time. Instead of a plateau of dusty emptiness, they were starting to see bushes and trees. Grass peeked out from the edges of rocks. Finn even thought she heard water flowing in the distance. It made her wonder if they'd get thirsty if they were out here for a long time. Or hungry?

It had never dawned on her to think of this like a camping trip, that they'd need supplies. What if she'd failed at that most basic of things—being prepared? As she ran through the list of ways she'd screwed this up, she realized she was cold. She looked back at Jed. He'd stuffed his hands in his pockets and drawn his arms tighter to his body.

Shit.

What if they didn't have enough clothing? What if they froze to death before they found Noah? Would they lapse into comas, too? Or if they died in their dreams, would they die in the real world?

She noticed the hummingbird had stopped moving forward. He was just buzzing back and forth in his giant U-shape right in front of her. She stood still and watched a moment, wondering what she was supposed to do.

Why wasn't there a manual for this?

She was really cold.

Jed stood next to her, watching the hummingbird. He started to whistle.

He had the craziest whistle. He would pick a note and stay with that note, jumping up and down octaves. Not quite a song, more a musical exercise. He did it when they studied. It had the advantage of not being distracting; it was calming, like a meditation. Jed pulled his hands out of his pockets and stood, whistling, matching the duration of his notes to the arc of the hummingbird as it zoomed back and forth.

Finn wasn't quite as cold as she'd been the moment before.

Why?

She listened to Jed whistle, thought about how safe it made her feel, and suddenly she knew that her fear was part of the trap. The long walk full of nothingness, lots of time to think. And she was, about all the ways this could go wrong. If she gave in to those thoughts, she and Jed were doomed. Hungry, thirsty, cold, chased by wolves. Her fear would manifest all of it—well, maybe not the wolves. Maybe something worse. She could make it happen. She could create nightmares. For both of them.

They had everything they needed. They had prepared in every way they needed to. She listened to Jed whistle and looked at the hummingbird. It was smiling at her. Not in a friendly way. It was like that cat in Alice in Wonderland. She held out her hand, and a rock appeared in it. She bounced it up and down like a tennis ball. She meant for it to be threatening. It worked, because the hummingbird stopped smiling.

"Get moving," she told the bird.

The trees grew thicker; limbs drooped ominously close to the ground. They reminded her of the trees she'd seen in the little girl's nightmare. She put an arm to Jed's elbow and steered him to the middle of the path, just in case. Every now and then, the hummingbird disappeared. Finn wondered where it was going. Was it getting instructions or hoping she'd step off the path and follow it into the forest? She wasn't going to. There were too many fairy tales involving children wandering into the dark forest for her not to take seriously the uneasy feeling in the pit of her stomach.

As she and Jed stood waiting for the hummingbird to come back, Jed put an arm around her. "Does this count as a date?"

"Yes. If you're going for the worst date ever."

"I will call that a no, because that was not my goal." When she laughed but didn't say anything, he said, "What do we do if that bird doesn't come back?"

"I don't know. Even if it does, I wonder if we should leave and come back another time."

"Why would we do that?"

"We've been walking forever. What are your parents going to say if you don't wake up in the morning?" Finn asked him.

"I never thought about that."

What if the hummingbird didn't come back? Finn thought back

to Sydney's black grouse. It led him to a tunnel. As much as she didn't want to walk into the woods, Finn wondered if perhaps the humming-bird disappeared because it had taken her as far as it could. "Jed," Finn whispered. "Do me a favor, make a slow circle with your light."

Jed twirled. The first time, Finn didn't see anything. The trees were too thick. "Can you go lower?" He got down on one knee and spun around again. It was so dark the forest was absorbing the light. "One more time. Slower." He spun around again, so slowly he was barely moving. It was just blackness and then—

"Wait."

Jed stopped.

"Back up a little bit."

He spun back.

"I know it sounds weird, but it's darker there than it is on either the left or the right, isn't it?"

Jed swung his head left and right. "Yeah," he said. "It's like the light is being eaten, which sounds pretty ominous now that I've said it out loud."

Indeed. And, since they were walking into a trap, that meant it was probably exactly where they were supposed to be headed.

Finn had kept the rock she'd created, rolling it around in her hand as they walked. Now that she was standing at the edge of what seemed like a tunnel, but one without any visible structure, it felt like the logical thing to do was to hurl it into the darkness. So she did. And, as it pierced the blackness, the rock disappeared. There was no sound of it hitting the ground or anything else.

"Not going to lie; that seems weird," Jed said.

Finn held her hand up to the spot where the blackness began and then, after a moment, tentatively took her pinkie finger and pushed it through. The buzzing was louder than she'd ever heard it. She yanked back her finger. Jed jumped back, too, startled.

"Something bite you?" he asked.

"No. I just . . . I got nervous." Finn took a moment and then turned to Jed. "I think this is . . . I don't know, some kind of vortex of evil."

"Don't sugarcoat it, Finn."

"I don't know what else to call it. I think this is a good moment for you to wake up and go home."

"Nope."

She looked in his eyes. "Serious" wasn't one of his looks. But right now, he looked serious.

She pointed to the darkness. "I think the Sorcerer feeds on fear." Jed's eyebrows lifted. "He needs nightmares. If we go in here, it'll be like a waking nightmare. You'll feel fear, hear it. But you cannot give in to it. Whatever you have to do, think of wool socks or milkshakes or—"

All of a sudden her mind was blank. She couldn't think of any happy things.

"You?" he said, smiling.

"Oh my God. That is so cheesy. It's beneath you."

"But you're smiling."

"Your ridiculousness makes me laugh."

"I will think of happy things. If I'm not, remind me. And I will do the same for you. Which is why it's good we are here together."

He had a point. She grabbed his hand. He squeezed hers. She turned back to the darkness.

"What if we don't find him, Jed?"

"That's not happy."

"But what . . . what if we're too late? What if he's gone or beyond saving?"

"We will deal with that when we have to. Right now, I believe he's waiting for us, counting on us. Well, you. That's why he came into your dream. He knew you were the one who could help him, even if he didn't know what kind of help he needed."

What if Jed was wrong? She couldn't will herself to go into the darkness. One step, she said to herself. Just take one step. But she couldn't.

Until she felt Jed squeeze her hand. Without saying a word, he stepped forward, pulling her with him.

The cold hit her like a hammer. She couldn't see anything; the light from Jed's headlamp was gone. It was dark, so dark. She even felt her Lochran straining to stay lit. The only sound was the buzzing, so loud it crushed every other possible sound.

It wasn't clear which way was forward or backward or up or down.

Her mind filled . . .

Images . . .

Snow. Father's funeral. Ambulance ride—hospital, Noah, eyes closed. Pale. Mother . . . airport. Snap pain—cast. Neighbor dog. Blood, blood, blood—

"Stop!" she screamed, though she wasn't sure if she was saying it inside her head or outside.

But it wouldn't stop.

More images pushed through.

Nana, dead, lying in an open casket. Noah's hand outstretched but out of reach. Her father's airplane falling,

falling,

falling,

out of the sky and into the cold lake.

She felt something against her wrist. Saint Patrick pressing into her skin as Jed squeezed her hand. Jed still holding on.

Those last images. Nana . . . Noah . . . her dad. Those weren't her memories. Something, someone was pushing them into her mind. Her knees were shaking. She felt like she was going to collapse. If she did, she knew she'd never get up. "No!" she screamed, and this time, she heard herself saying it.

She had to fight back, clear her mind, and—

Remember.

Nana's last birthday, the lopsided cake Finn had baked for her.

Noah playing ice hockey on the pond at the park.

Jed, wearing the too-small Chelsea jersey she'd ordered from the UK.

She held Jed's hand as tightly as she could.

"Jed!" she screamed. "Tell me your favorite element." He didn't answer. She forced herself to take a step and pulled him with her. "Mint chip ice cream, green or no?" He felt less like a deadweight, as he'd taken a step on his own. "I'd like to go to the prom with you. Should we go to the prom?"

And, just like that, they stepped from the dark void and into . . . a cave. There was the faint odor of rotting garbage. Jed's headlamp was working again, the light steady on some rocks in front of them, including the one she'd thrown through the tunnel.

Finn turned to Jed. He was still, eyes glassy, his cheeks streaked with tears.

"Are you okay?" When he didn't answer, Finn reached up and put her hands on his face. She tilted it down so he was looking at her. "Jed?" He still wasn't there. "You are brave, strong, and I am so glad you are here." She stood on her tiptoes and kissed him. She held it until she felt him kiss her back. Bit by bit, she felt the warmth return to his lips. And, then, after a moment, he wrapped his arms around her. He ended the kiss and buried his head in her hair.

He mumbled something. She couldn't make out what it was.

"What did you say?" Finn whispered.

He leaned back and looked her in the face. "Worst. Date. Ever."

THIRTY-TWO

Julia stared at the ceiling, trying to find benign farm animals in the shadows created by the light at the edge of the curtains. When she squinted, one of them looked like a sheep, but finding it hadn't made her any more tired than counting sheep, or meditating, or singing children's nursery rhymes.

She didn't want to sleep. She wanted to go into Finn's room and watch her, help her, make sure that she got through the night okay. But deep down, Julia knew going into Finn's room wasn't a good idea. She'd stared at a comatose Noah enough nights to know that just sitting wasn't going to give anyone comfort.

And there was always the risk that she might actually screw things up for her daughter. What if she sneezed and woke Finn, would that put her in danger? Could Julia do anything, positively or negatively, to affect what was happening . . . wherever Finn was? She had no idea. She wished she'd asked Conor more questions when he was alive, forced him to explain the

Dreamwalker world to her. She wished she'd thought to ask how they'd know if their children were Dreamwalkers, but she hadn't. You could put it on the list of the many ways she had failed her children. Or at least felt she'd failed her children. She hoped they didn't feel that way, but, like the Dreamwalking questions so long ago, it wasn't one she'd ever had the courage to ask.

She threw her feet off the side of the bed. She was awake. Better to be awake someplace else.

As she headed to the kitchen to make a cup of chamomile tea, Julia glanced out the front window to see if it was snowing. It wasn't. But there was a car sitting in front of the house. It was running; she could see smoke curling up from the tailpipe. She crossed to the window. Someone was inside in the driver's seat. It was too dark to see them.

Julia went to the door and flipped on the outside light. When she went back to the window, there was just enough light to see who was inside the car . . .

Rafe.

The grass crunched under her boots as she walked across the lawn. It was cold, and the blanket she'd wrapped around herself was barely able to keep it out.

Rafe had looked her way when she'd opened the front door and watched her as she walked toward him. When she got close to the car, he leaned over and opened the passenger door. Julia slid inside, comforted by how warm the car was, even though she'd been outside for less than a minute.

"How long have you been sitting out here?" Julia asked him.

"Not long. Maybe an hour. Two."

"What exactly are you doing?"

"Same thing as you. Waiting. Wishing I could help."

Julia watched a scrap of paper skitter across the road in front of them. It hit the curb and fell to the ground.

"I'm scared," she said, as much to fill the silence as to tell him.

Rafe didn't respond. He just reached over and took her hand in his.

THIRTY-THREE

Finn turned and looked at the cave wall behind them. The void, the tunnel—or door, she wasn't sure what it was exactly. What she did know was that it was hard to see on this side and that when they got back here from wherever they were going, she wasn't sure she'd be able to find it.

"Can I borrow that knife I gave you?"

Jed reached into his pocket and pulled out the Swiss Army knife. Finn moved her hand about an inch over the cave wall until she found a place that was colder than the rest. She didn't want to touch it; she didn't want those thoughts back, if she didn't have to have them. She picked up a small pebble and threw it at the wall. It disappeared. The entrance was there, just invisible.

She scraped in the wall an arrow pointing to it. And then, just to be safe, she drew one on the ground, too. And then a third on a large rock farther away. Jed's headlamp followed her progress, so she knew he was watching. "We don't know who's in here and how badly they won't want us to find our way out," she explained.

"Oh, I'm guessing pretty badly."

"So better safe than sorry."

"I hate that expression. Like you can't be safe and sorry." The headlamp arced around the vastness of the cave. "What now?" The light threw a faint beam into the distance, highlighting ripples on a pool of water. Finn raised her hand, and a blue light came to life on her palm. It dwarfed the light of Jed's headlamp, and now it was possible to see just how big the cave was.

And the water . . . less a pool than a lake. A giant lake.

Shit.

Finn hated water, so of course it was obvious what they had to do. She pointed at the giant, dark lake. "I think we go swimming," she said.

The ripples in the water were caused by a black tarry substance falling from stalactites on the roof of the cave. Finn held out her blue light, but it couldn't penetrate the surface. The lake was just dark and imposing, like the void they'd found in the forest. She cautiously dipped one finger into it. To her surprise, it was just cold. No wave of fear assaulted her.

Finn saw Jed's beam of light moving over the surface. "Sydney Norwich swam in the pool. Then he found the maze and . . ." Nothing followed. Finn thought he'd probably just remembered how it ended for Sydney. Not good.

"Yeah," she said.

And then it hit her.

She'd forgotten the map of the maze. All the time they'd spent studying it and trying to figure out what it meant, and she'd left it behind. She'd packed a photo of her and Noah but didn't bring the only thing they needed. They couldn't go into the maze without it. Even if the maze led nowhere, they needed to know its shape so they could get out. If they got lost, she could rip her Lochran and go home, just like Sydney and Rafe. But Jed . . . he'd be stuck there forever, probably end up in a coma like Noah. And without the Lochran, she wouldn't be able to save either of them.

They had to turn back.

All their time and effort wasted. Finn fought to keep herself from bursting into tears.

"Oh, Jed. I've made a terrible mis—"

She turned around. Jed's lamp was focused on the piece of paper in his hands. The light of the lamp projected the image through the paper.

It was a copy of the maze.

"You brought the maze," she gasped as a wave of relief washed over her.

"And my notes." He held it out. She saw tiny scrawls all over the page. "What were you saying?"

"Thank you."

"That's not what you were saying. It started with 'm-i-s.'"

"I'll tell you later. Ready to go swimming?"

"I think the better question is, are you ready to go swimming?"

The answer was always no, but Finn took his hand and stepped into the water.

THIRTY-FOUR

Jed had taken an extra step so he'd be at the same level as her, and his headlamp created a little bubble of light around them, but there was nothing to see. Finn stood still for a moment, holding her breath. Sydney had been able to breathe underwater. She knew that. It was still hard to let go of her instinct to hold her breath.

She hated water. At least, anything bigger than a bath. Hated it.

Jed turned toward her. He was holding his breath, too. He puffed his cheeks out like a puffer fish and raised his eyebrows. What now? his face said.

Finn's lungs burned. She held on to the breath until she couldn't anymore and then opened her mouth. And—

Nothing. It was almost like the water wasn't water. Like it was liquid air. She could feel that it was in her mouth, but it felt fine. She breathed through her nose. That was fine, too. Jed exhaled and then breathed.

He gave Finn a thumbs-up, and they headed deeper into the darkness.

* * *

They'd only gone a short distance when Jed's light bounced off a bright surface. A golden door embedded in a giant silver wall. The light from his lamp kept bouncing, eventually lighting up the entire area around them. After a moment, it was almost as bright as daylight.

"Holy cow, that's cool," Jed said, surprised.

"We can talk," Finn said, equally surprised. Sydney had been alone; he probably hadn't tried to talk. "Is that the entrance to the maze?"

Jed held up their drawing. The door was in the right place. "Hard to know. From here, it looks like it could be."

"Well then, I guess there's nothing to do but go in."

"No."

Surprised, she turned to look at him. Had he finally had enough?

He quickly continued. "Okay, trust me, I'm not going to stay out here by myself and be monster bait. I just need a minute. I'm . . . I'm having lots of feelings. Fear, confusion, amazement . . . hunger. Though, if I'm completely honest, I'm always hungry." They stood looking at the door for a moment before he continued. "Do you think I'll remember this when I wake up?"

Finn didn't know. She was just hoping they'd both wake up; she hadn't given any thought to what would happen when they did.

"I don't know. But I promise I'll tell you about it if you don't."

"I'm not going to believe you." He took a deep breath, or whatever it was they were doing with the liquid air. "I'm ready."

Finn opened the golden door. The water stopped at the edge, like a wall. She stepped out of the water and into the maze. The sun shone brightly. They had reached the promised land.

Finn pulled her sword from its sheath. She saw the look of awe on Jed's face. They started walking, and it didn't take long to get to the first decision point.

"We know there's no exit to this maze, so what exactly are we doing?"

"I'm not one hundred percent sure."

"Inspirational leadership, Finn."

"I mean . . . why have a maze? To trap people? Maybe. In which case, keep your Swiss Army knife at the ready. But could be it's like the Minotaur."

"So we are looking for the spawn of Poseidon's great white bull."

"Hidden in a maze to keep it from eating everyone in your kingdom." Finn used her sword to cut an arrow in the floor to help them find their way out.

"You think there's something hidden in the maze?"

"I don't know," she said. She knew uncertainty wasn't very motivating, but honesty seemed more important than guessing at this point.

"Okay." He pulled out his Swiss Army knife and opened it. "Let's go find it."

She laughed. "Don't hurt yourself."

They moved carefully, marking their route just as Sydney Norwich had done. The material that made the long passageways changed

as they went: thatch, wood, stone, brick, bronze, iron. There were
gouges and scratches in some of them. Finn wondered what had
made them. She reached and touched a long slash on the wall.

"No!"

Startled, she turned to Jed. "What?"

"I didn't say anything."

The voice had been inside her head. She turned back to the slash
and touched it again and—

A spiked metal ball struck the wall, sending a shower of
sparks over the Sorcerer. He backed up, his Lochran stick high
to protect his head. A tall man with long blond hair advanced
on him, swinging the iron ball menacingly. There was a Lochran
around his neck. It blazed with an orange light. The Sorcerer
retreated slowly.

Finn pulled her fingers from the gouge. Farther down in an area
that was wood, not stone, she saw a deeper gouge. She walked over,
touched it and—

The tall man swung the mace. The Sorcerer jumped out of
the way, and the mace hit the wall again. But this time, instead
of bouncing off, the studded ball stuck in the wood. The tall
man yanked on it to no avail, and from within the horned animal's skull, the Sorcerer's eyes smiled as he stepped forward. His
Lochran stick made a long arc and—

Finn pulled her fingers from this deeper gouge. She didn't want
to watch that Dreamwalker die. Or whatever happened to a Dream-
walker when they lost.

Jed was watching her.

"What is it?"

"Nothing," she lied.

"Finn?" It was clear he didn't believe her.

"We . . . we need to be careful."

"That's like a character in a movie saying, 'What could possibly go wrong?' Guaranteed to be ironically prescient."

She could hear the worry in his voice. Fear was the enemy. She had to remember that. "I don't think anyone in the history of the world knows as much about this guy as we do. But still, we're sixteen years old and he's fifteen thousand. He's had a lot more time to practice being evil than we've had to practice being heroic," she said, smiling.

Jed didn't smile back. He just looked back at his maze drawing and made a left. Finn marked an arrow on the floor and followed him.

She checked over her shoulder to make sure they weren't being followed.

There were fewer scratches in the walls the deeper into the maze they got. Could be that fewer Dreamwalkers got this far. Or the walls were too hard to register the battles they'd fought. Since the Sorcerer was still around, it probably meant he always came out on top.

Jed stopped. "The center of the maze is that way," he said, gesturing to the left.

"Okay. You stay here."

"No way."

"Please. It could be a trap. Let me just check it out first." Finn handed him her sword. "You protect the rear flank." She saw his smile reflected in the mirrored blade as he waved the sword back and forth.

"And, of course, when you say 'protect the rear flank,' you mean..."

"Don't hurt yourself," they said together.

Finn took a few tentative steps forward. She didn't hear anything. If the Sorcerer was waiting, he was doing it very quietly. She sniffed the air. There was none of that sulfur odor she'd smelled the other times she'd confronted him. She continued around the edge of a wall and into a room.

Empty, except for a pile of weaponry in a corner and a large, flat rock in the center. Finn glanced at the weapons: swords, spears, maces, crossbows, guns. Weapons from every era of human history. Undoubtedly weapons of Dreamwalkers who had found the maze before her. What had Sydney carried? Which one was Noah's? She wondered if she should try to find it so she could give it back to him. Probably not, she decided.

She walked to the flat rock in the center of the room. There was a stick resting on top of it: small, worn smooth from someone holding it. A leather string at the top was wrapped around the shaft of a black feather that had lost much of its plumage. It reminded Finn of objects she'd seen in her shaman research; spiritual leaders had used these kinds of objects to heal the sick and chase away evil spirits. They were sources of power for shamans.

It looked old.

And here it was: in the middle of dream-nowhere, protected by voids and lakes and a crazy maze. It meant something to the Sorcerer. Maybe it was like King Arthur's sword or the Holy Grail. She wasn't sure exactly. She just knew it was important.

Finn picked it up.

THIRTY-FIVE

Noah heard the monster scream. As the sound rippled through the darkness, barely a whisper, it was clear the creature was far away, but Noah was still surprised to realize he didn't feel the fear he usually did. Everything about the creature used to fill him with a life-sucking dread. But not now.

Why?

He listened as the monster's cry echoed into silence.

Noah sensed that the monster was scared. What could it possibly be afraid of?

Noah didn't know.

For the first time in a long time, though, he felt a twinge of hope. Just a little.

Enough.

He took a deep breath. He'd be ready, whenever the hope got here.

THIRTY-SIX

Finn heard the roar and rushed out of the room to find Jed looking down the hallway, sword raised.

"Was that you?"

Jed shook his head. "It came from over—"

He took one of his hands off the sword to point in the direction the scream had come from, but as he did, the sword tilted toward him. Finn reached out to stop it from slicing into his arm, and the blade cut across her hand. Saint Patrick was covered in blood.

"Oh God, Finn. I'm so sorry."

"I'm fine." She took the sword and leaned it against her legs.

"No, you're hurt. You—"

"Jed, the scream."

Jed indicated an adjacent wall. "It came from over there. It sounded far away. Muffled almost. Was that him?" He sawed at his T-shirt with his Swiss Army knife until he had ripped a strip from the bottom.

"I think so." She pulled the shaman's stick out of the pocket where she'd shoved it. "It happened after I picked this up."

"A talking stick?"

"Sure what it looks like."

He wrapped the T-shirt strip around the cut on her hand. "Dude's not happy you took it."

"We need to find him before he finds us. Can I see the map?" Jed handed her the maze drawing. "If it came from over there, that's the opposite direction from the maze's entrance." Jed nodded in agreement. "Do we have to go all the way back to the front door and hope we can get around?" Finn wondered aloud, hoping it wasn't true.

Jed was silent a moment, then took the map out of her hands. "Follow me."

He ran off, Swiss Army knife in hand. Finn tucked the stick back into her pocket, picked up her sword, and chased after him.

When Jed took a left, instead of following the arrow they'd marked, Finn couldn't help herself.

"Do you know what—"

Without stopping, he called out, "Sort of. Trust me."

She did. And they had the map. If they got lost, they could wander around until they found one of their arrows and go the direction indicated. Not a problem, unless the Sorcerer came into the maze looking for them.

It didn't take a rocket scientist to know he was pissed off. They needed to get out of here, because the longer they were here, the greater the chance he'd find them. Finn didn't want her sword and Jed's Swiss Army knife to end up on the pile in the center room.

Jed stopped in front of a blank wall.

"I think this is it."

"What?"

"I had a dream." Jed was trying to remember something. She could tell because his eyes were closed and his eyebrows were scrunched together. He almost stabbed himself in the face with the Swiss Army knife. "There were... what were they? Walking..."

Finn knew what he was talking about. "Ants."

"Yes, yes. Ants. They were walking in the maze, and I opened up a new exit for them. I don't know why I think it'll work, but I do."

Finn remembered his dream. She'd walked into it as Jed broke through the sand maze with his finger, and the wall in front of them did look like some sort of earthen material.

"So what do we—"

But before she could finish, Jed reared up and judo-kicked the wall. Almost as quickly, the wall started to collapse as the force of Jed's blow reverberated through it, like a sandcastle when the tide came in. When it finally stopped crumbling, they were standing in front of a huge hole that opened into...

Another cave.

One that was bigger than the one where they'd found the lake.

All over the walls, there were drawings, just like the ones Finn had seen from the caves in Europe. Pictures of animals—birds, wolves, mountain lions, deer, and buffalo—and, all around them, stick-figure hunters. Finn scanned the walls until she found what she was looking for, a human figure wearing a buffalo head.

The Sorcerer.

She pulled out the picture of the cave painting from her pocket.

It was a perfect match. This was his space, his home. He'd been decorating these walls for a long time. Brown and ochre images filled the spaces between openings in the cave walls.

Openings.

Tunnels. Or more caves.

There were hundreds of them, all filled with impenetrable darkness.

"Man," Jed said after a moment. "This dude really likes caves."

Somewhere in one of these tunnels was Noah. Finn could feel it. He was waiting for her. She also knew that in another tunnel or maybe in Noah's tunnel, the Sorcerer was racing in her direction, angry she had stolen his precious . . . stick.

As if he knew what she was thinking, another scream shot out of the blackness. This one was closer. Louder. Angrier.

They were running out of time. They had to find Noah. Maybe more light would help. She tried to create the blue light in her hand. Nothing happened. Maybe she was just nervous. She closed her eyes and tried again. Before she opened her eyes, she knew she had failed again. She jumped, hoping to fly toward the ceiling. She cleared about four inches.

"What are you doing?" Jed asked.

She had her sword. Jed had his headlamp and knife. They had what they'd brought, but it seemed the Sorcerer had created a world that stripped Dreamwalkers of their powers. It must limit his powers, too. Otherwise, Finn didn't know why he wouldn't have popped up as soon as they got here.

So maybe they had a little time until he found them, but Finn would be in deep shit when he did because her real abilities were pretty damn limited. They had to find Noah and get out of there before that happened.

But how? There were hundreds of tunnels. Finn tried to remember Sydney's book and the notes from the monastery. What was she missing?

A long moment passed.

The scream had faded away. All Finn could hear was Jed's breathing.

In. Out. In. Out.

And it came to her.

Malum. Evil. The eel. The void. The odor. The cold. The buzzing.

The Sorcerer survived by stealing Lochrans from Dreamwalkers and roamed through the dream space creating fear. He was the King of Nightmares. He needed people to feel scared and alone, isolated from all that was good around them; he drove them to violence and fed off the energy that rippled from all that chaos.

To find Noah, to defeat the darkness, Finn had to be everything the Sorcerer was not. Her power was that spark inside her that connected her to everything and everyone. The Lochran was a representation of that spark.

And she suddenly knew that the Sorcerer could not take it from her. She could destroy it or give it away. But it had to be her choice.

If she stayed calm and connected, she could find Noah and get all of them out of there.

"Jed, turn off your light."

"Really?"

"Yes."

Jed flipped off the light, and it got darker than even Finn expected.

She untucked her shirt. Her Lochran threw off enough light to see where she was walking. She crossed to one of the openings in the cave wall. She stood in front of it, trying to see with her whole body, to listen with her soul, to find a connection to her brother.

Nothing.

She stepped to the next opening and did the same thing. Nothing. She stepped to another one. Nothing.

Another roar echoed through the space in front of her. He was getting closer. She quickly moved to the next tunnel.

Nothing.

Finn kept moving.

Nothing.

Nothing.

Nothing.

Jed stayed close. She was sure he had no idea what she was doing. She wasn't really sure, either. She just prayed that when she got to the right tunnel, she'd—

Her Lochran started pulsing.

Ba-boom. Ba-boom. Ba-boom.

It was a heartbeat. Noah's heartbeat.

"He's here," she said to Jed before running into the darkness of the tunnel.

THIRTY-SEVEN

Finn's Lochran got brighter the farther into the tunnel she went. She wondered if she should slow down. The Sorcerer was looking for her. If she slowed down, at least she might see him before he saw her, but if she slowed down, he might also—

Her foot hit something, and she tumbled to the ground. Her sword skittered away, and the cave floor pulled at the strip of Jed's T-shirt on her hand. Her wound scraped against the ground. She bit back a sob just in time to hear a cry behind her. Something was here.

She whipped around.

Noah, barely visible by the light of her Lochran.

She'd run right into him.

She felt the fears she'd been holding—that her brother couldn't be saved, that even if he could, she couldn't do it—flood through her. She let them go.

Because here he was.

"Noah," she whispered as she scrambled to him.

She was overcome with joy, sadness, fear, wonder, anger,

confusion. She was feeling everything she'd ever felt all at once. Until after a moment, everything faded away, except relief.

"Noah," she whispered again, wrapping her arms around him, tears running down her cheeks.

"Finn," he whispered back.

Finn brushed the hair from his eyes and made a bloody smear on his forehead. Her hand was bleeding,

"I heard two sets of feet," Noah whispered to Finn nervously. Only now did Finn hear the rattle in his throat.

"That was me."

Noah tilted his head, confused. "Jed? How did you—"

Another howl blasted down the dark tunnel.

"Long story," Finn blurted out. "We'll tell you when we're safe." She pulled Noah to his feet and picked up her sword.

"We can't leave yet; we need—" Noah started.

"Noah, we've got to go."

"Finn, please. We need to find Dad. He's alive."

Alive?

Before she could respond, Jed gently said, "Noah, you've been here a long time, maybe—"

"He's alive, Jed," Noah protested.

Another howl echoed through the tunnel.

Finn willed her heart to stop pounding. That's why Noah had put himself in all this danger. He was just a boy who missed his dead father. She wanted to comfort him, as she had so many times, but they were still in danger.

"We can't stay here," she said firmly. "We'll talk about it later."

"It's the truth, Finn. It is." She could feel the longing in his voice.

"Okay. But that monster's coming, and you're in no shape to do anything. So Jed's going to get you out of here."

Jed's head jerked in Finn's direction. "What?"

Finn's plan. She'd gone over the details a thousand times.

"It's the only way we can all get home," she said as she gently stretched her Lochran. "I can take you back to the River and wake you up. You'll be in your own bed. I can wake myself up and be in my own bed. But Noah . . . without a Lochran, he's trapped. It's why he's in the coma. It's why he's getting weaker all the time."

She wriggled the Lochran off her hips and stepped out of it. She put it over Noah's head and then shoulders, sliding it to his waist so she could cover it with his T-shirt.

"It's not mine," Noah protested.

"We're all connected. It'll work." Noah looked better already.

Jed grabbed Finn's arm. "I'm not going to leave you here."

"I need to borrow this." She leaned the sword against her leg and peeled the headlamp off his head. She put it on and then ran her fingers through his matted hair. Mostly to fix it, but also so she could touch him. In case . . .

"It's the only way, Jed. You've got to get Noah through the maze, a lake, and that void. You'll need time." She kissed him lightly on the lips. He tasted salty. Sweat, tears, probably both. They'd lived a lifetime today. "Get to the River. Please. Take Noah home. I will see you later." She started to head off.

"How? You don't have a Lochran."

She could hear how scared Jed was, but there wasn't time to explain it. But Noah knew.

"She's going to get my Lochran back," she heard Noah say. "She's going to take it from the monster."

THIRTY-EIGHT

Finn ran hard until the tunnel curved and she was out of sight. She stopped to look back, just to make sure Jed and Noah were leaving. It took a moment, but the faint light of her Lochran finally started moving away. She took a deep breath, tried to still her heart. What Noah had said...

Their father. Poor Noah had wanted him to be alive so badly; it had been easy for the Sorcerer to trap him.

When the light of her Lochran disappeared, Finn turned and headed deeper into the tunnel. She felt the Saint Patrick medal flicking back and forth on her wrist. "I'll be praying for you," Sharon had said. Finn wondered if prayers had a shelf life.

The Sorcerer roared again. It was loud enough to make Finn stop. He was close. She tucked herself into a spot against the wall. She just had to delay him long enough for Jed and Noah to get through the void. After that, well...

Finn shook the worry out of her head. She had a plan. Stick to the plan.

She touched the headlamp to make sure it was facing forward. She gripped her sword firmly in both hands.

She could hear water dripping in the cave.

She wondered about this place. He'd obviously created it, a kind of lucid dreaming that allowed him to fabricate a space of his own. A place that must resemble the French cave he had called home all those years ago.

And now, who knew how many other Dreamwalkers he'd captured, only to leave them rotting in these tunnels. How many had died in the real world, as their spirits slowly wilted away in the darkness, the way Noah was on the verge of doing? How she would if she couldn't find a Lochran and get out of there.

They'd all come here, as she had, on their own missions, hoping they could use their skills to conquer... what the hell was he?

A walking nightmare?

A fifteen-thousand-year-old nightmare. And she was a sixteen-year-old high school sophomore. That did not seem like a fair fight.

Maybe instead of fight, the Sorcerer would agree to a dance contest. She was sure she was a better dancer than he was. The idea cheered her up, but only for a moment, because then a hint of sulfur wafted through the tunnel. The plop, plop, plop of the water was replaced by a louder thud of feet on the tunnel floor.

He was here.

She held her breath.

Thud, thud...

Almost.

THUD.

Now!

She hit the On button of the headlamp and leaped from her hiding place.

The Sorcerer turned away, knocking into the wall in surprise.

Finn swung her sword at the Lochran stick, breaking his grip and sending the stick skittering down the tunnel. As quickly as she could, she swung her sword again, but he was a step faster and jumped back. Her blade sliced through air.

Finn's follow-through carried her arms across her body, and he jumped at her now exposed side.

She felt a searing pain on her forearm as a flaming sore singed her skin. The sword fell from her hand, the grip too slippery with her blood to hang on to it. The clatter as it hit the floor reverberated through the tunnel.

She heard him more than she saw him racing toward her. She quickly got to her feet and, like they'd done during the parkour unit in gym class, jumped up against the wall and pushed off with her foot. He barely missed her, but his momentum carried him right to her sword. He picked it up and turned around to face her.

He was a weird sight. The antlered head. Skin clothes. No shoes. Flaming sores. And the smell, like a plate full of rotten eggs.

Horrible.

The Sorcerer waved the sword back and forth, savoring the moment. The sulfur stench filled her nostrils as her lamplight bounced off his eyes. They were cold and dark. Just like . . .

Finn flashed to—

Her father looking through the hole the night Finn was trapped in the box. His dark eyes glaring at her.

The sulfur smell had been there.

She couldn't think about this now, but she couldn't help but flash to—

Her dream.

The one Noah was in, when he fought the Sorcerer. There was a shadow in the background. Finn looks, sees her father. Moving away from the fight, not toward it to help Noah. Why would her father be with the Sorcerer? And why was Conor in the dream world at all? He'd ripped his . . .

And then she saw it, around her father's wrist, a Lochran worn like a bracelet.

He lied.

He didn't rip off his Lochran. And, if he lied about that—

It took all of Finn's willpower to stay upright, be focused on the monster in front of her.

Inside the mask, she saw wrinkles form on the edge of the Sorcerer's eyes. He was smiling. He could sense her struggle and thought the battle was already won. She needed to get a grip, or it would be true.

She needed to get back to Noah.

Another sore burst through the skin on the back of his hand. It hissed and then started burning with a steady flame. The smell. It was overpowering.

"Where's my father? What did you do with my father?" The questions exploded out of Finn.

He responded with a series of guttural sounds she couldn't interpret. She'd understood the language of the Asian Dreamwalker, but this, this was . . . old, she thought. Just like him. Even if he wanted to answer her question, she wouldn't understand what he said.

He took a step closer.

Finn backed up, glancing at his Lochran-covered staff. No way she could get to it without being sliced in half.

He took another step forward.

The entrance to the tunnel was at her back. Could she outrun him if she turned and . . . no. She knew she couldn't.

She had to stand and fight. But with what? All she had was . . .

The talking stick.

Finn reached into her back pocket and pulled it out. He froze. She saw the monster's eyes widen.

She put a hand on either end, pretending that she was going to break it.

He screamed an unintelligible string of words. She guessed it was a version of "You break that and I will crush you like a bug." She didn't say anything. She simply pointed at the sword and gestured to the ground.

He yelled again, enraged.

She grabbed the mangy feather on the talking stick and pulled at it.

He stopped screaming. Finn pointed at the sword again and then the ground.

He put the sword down.

Finn made a waving gesture, indicating he should back up. And, *amazingly, he did. She wondered what kind of power this stick had. Whatever it was, today was not the day she would find out.*

Today was just the day she was going to get the hell out of there.

When he'd backed up far enough that she could get his Lochran staff without him rushing her, she picked it up. He hissed at her, like a snake. She shrugged, hoping that was the universal sign for "I don't give a shit."

She gestured toward the entrance of the tunnel and tapped the two pieces of wood together forcefully when he didn't move. He shook, having some sort of seizure, and moved immediately when she threatened to do it again.

Interesting.

Finn kept him fifteen feet in front of her so she'd have time to react if he decided to attack. She was starting to feel fuzzy. She'd tried to do some breathing exercises. They didn't help. She assumed it had something to do with giving her Lochran away. She found herself getting distracted, thinking about Noah and Jed and . . . her father, so she started studying his weapon, which had the added benefit of keeping her eyes forward and the Sorcerer in view.

There were eight Lochrans embedded in his stick: two blues, two greens, a red, an orange, a purple, and one that was the color of a wheat field. They were attached to the stick as if they had grown there. Where they connected to the stick was how a new branch con- nects to a tree limb. Finn was pretty sure they would snap off cleanly if she bent them near the root, and equally certain doing so would piss him off.

When they walked through the hole in the maze, Finn guided him to the entrance, following the arrows she'd cut into the floor. She wasn't exactly sure what she would do when they got to the wall of water. He'd created a giant lake in his dream world, so she assumed he was comfortable with water in a way she wasn't. She'd also noticed he'd started looking at her over his shoulder. No doubt, he had formulated some sort of surprise attack. You don't survive fifteen thousand years by doing what you're told.

"Hey," Finn said. He looked over his shoulder but didn't turn all the way around. Finn couldn't see his hands, and she suddenly realized she hadn't seen them in a while. His skin pants didn't have pockets, but it was possible there was a pouch underneath to hide something sharp. She saw his shoulders tense. She banged the Lochran-covered staff and the talking stick together in a rat-a-tat rhythm. He winced, so she did it again, hoping it would dissuade him from whatever he was planning.

It didn't.

The Sorcerer spun around and attacked.

Finn used the staff to deflect his arm and the sharpened piece of obsidian he thrust at her. His momentum carried him past her, but he quickly turned to attack again.

Before he could, Finn did the only thing she could think of: She hurled the talking stick as far as she could. He howled in anger and watched it arc over the wall. Before he could turn back to her, Finn lunged at him, Lochran-covered staff held high.

She aimed for his head.

He ducked, as she knew he would. She planted her front foot and swung her back foot at his now-lowered head.

It connected solidly. And even though she was kicking an

animal's skull, she heard a satisfying thump as the force of her blow caused his head to bounce off the inside of it.

She advanced again, bringing the Lochran-covered staff down on his back.

As it made contact, she heard something . . . like roars of approval from the Dreamwalkers whose Lochrans had finally gotten payback.

She raised the staff to hit him again, but the Sorcerer scurried away on his hands and knees, getting out of range before finally climbing to his feet. Finn took a step forward, forcing him into full retreat.

He limped down the passageway. The wound she'd just made on his back hissed and then erupted in flame just as he turned the corner.

She assumed he was going to retrieve the talking stick. She hoped it landed far enough away to buy her some time. With one final look to make sure he was really gone, Finn plunged into the wall of water.

She kicked her legs and headed for the surface. When she was a good distance from the golden door, she opened her hand. The feather from the talking stick floated out of it. She'd thrown the talking stick because she had to, but if she was forced to give it back to him, she wanted to at least try to make it less useful. Who knew if losing the feather could do that, but it had been all she could think of.

She watched the feather drift toward the bottom of the lake. It disappeared into darkness as she turned and swam for the surface with the glowing Lochrans to lead her way.

THIRTY-NINE

Finn climbed out of the lake, exhausted. She stumbled to the wall of the cave and looked for the marks she'd made to help find the entrance to the void. They were still there, along with other marks Jed and Noah had carved into the wall:

U.

R.

Then a downward-facing arrow, followed by an O.

It was signed Noah + Jed.

You Are Arrow O, *she thought. That's obviously not right. But she didn't have time to figure it out. She needed to get the hell out of there. She needed to get home.*

Finn had decided the lime-green Lochran was Noah's. She took a deep breath and snapped it. It came off clean. She gently pried the circle of the Lochran open and put it around her neck. She immediately felt better.

She didn't know what to do with the Lochran-covered staff. If she threw it in the lake, the Sorcerer would probably find it.

She could hide it in the River, but it seemed that would doom the Dreamwalkers he'd taken them from to whatever state they were in now. She had to protect the Lochrans, hide them. Somewhere safe.

She quickly snapped the remaining seven glowing necklaces off the stick and put them in her pockets. They were warm. She hurled the now bare wooden staff into the distance and turned to the cave wall.

She cleared her mind and stepped—

Into the void.

It was so much worse alone.

She saw her father, cruel eyes staring at her.

She had to keep moving.

Noah. Jed. They were on the other side. It was so black. And she was so tired. Did Noah get through? What if he didn't have the strength to . . . ?

Why did Jed write a message? What if that wasted time Noah didn't have? What if Noah didn't make it through the tunnel? What if . . . the message . . . why?

URDownwardArrowO. URDownwardPointingatMyFeetO. URDownWhereI'mStandingO. URDownHereO. URHereO.

You Are Hero.

Noah and Jed. They loved her. Noah and Jed wanted her to—

Finn forced herself to take a step forward. As the darkness pulled her backward, she took another step. Noah. Jed. Noah, Jed.

Noah—

* * *

And she burst into the forest.

She took a deep breath. The dread that was crushing her lifted.

She heard a humming and looked up to see the hummingbird land on a limb above her head. Finn smiled. "Thanks, but I don't need your help."

She closed her eyes and found herself—

Back in the River.

She took it in. The anxious buzzing had dimmed. She heard music and laughter. She let it wash over her a moment, then turned to the past dreams and stretched out her arms. She was pulled into a thin strip of Finn-ness, which took her to—

A dream she'd had a long time ago as a child, a happy dream. Eddie was just a puppy. She'd dreamed he could fly as she took him on a walk. The leash bobbed up and down as he took off and landed. It was all young Finn could do to keep the exuberant puppy from floating away. She saw her dream playing out in front of her, the colors muted but all the elements recognizable. There was a tree on the parkway. It was still on their street today: old and gnarly, but beautiful. It had a crevasse running through its center where it had been touched by lightning a long time ago. The tree had lived, scarred, to tell its story. Finn removed the Lochrans from her pockets and put them inside the crevasse. She hoped they would be safe until she figured out how to help the Dreamwalkers they belonged to. Later.

Just how she'd find her father, if he were there to be found.
She closed her eyes and went—

Back to the River.

It was time to go home.

FORTY

Finn woke up in her room. Her head hurt. Her arms and legs—

Noah!

She jumped out of bed, winced as her feet hit the floor. Everything ached, but she had to see Noah. She raced down the hall to his room. He was on the bed, eyes closed. Eddie was sitting, facing the bed, almost waiting for something. She crossed over to Noah's bedside, her heart beating so quickly.

Please, let him be okay.

She took his hand, and a pain shot up her arm. She looked at her palm and found an angry red cut across it.

All the hurt was worth it if she'd brought Noah home. She pulled his hand to her cheek. It felt warm. She hoped he didn't have a fever.

"Noah," she said urgently.

Why wasn't he awake?

Was she wrong about everything? Was there no way to get

him out of his coma? A tear slipped down her cheek. Had all of it been for nothing?

"Noah," she whispered.

She held her breath.

Waited.

Nothing happened.

FORTY-ONE

The car was still running, but despite that, it had gotten cold a long time ago.

Julia and Rafe had talked for a long time: about his life as a Dreamwalker, his life since. She was glad to hear it, glad to know more about what Conor had gone through. After a while, he'd fallen asleep, had barely moved since, as if not dreaming had stilled his whole body.

When his hand had relaxed, she'd pulled it away to tuck it under the blanket for warmth. She just sat, waiting. She wasn't sure for what, until she saw Finn run across the kitchen toward Noah's room.

"Rafe," she said, already opening her door.

He was immediately awake and moving.

They rushed inside.

Dear God, Julia prayed, *please let them be okay.*

FORTY-TWO

Finn heard the front door open and was surprised when both her mother and Rafe rushed into Noah's room. Julia crossed to Finn and wrapped her arms around Finn's head, pulling it tight to her chest.

"I'm so happy to see you," Julia said. Finn waited for her mother to ask about Noah, but she didn't. She just held on, like she was afraid Finn would disappear if she let go.

"Mom . . . ," Finn whispered.

"Yes, Fionnuala."

Her mother hadn't called her that in a long time. Not since she was a little girl.

"He's not waking up, Mom. I don't know what else to do."

Her mother let go. "Get Nana. If there's anything that will help, she'll know what it is." As Finn walked by, Rafe gently touched her shoulder before moving to Noah's bedside.

* * *

Finn woke Nana. She sat up. "What happened?" she asked.

"I don't know, Nana. He's not waking up. I . . ." Finn dropped her head, swallowed by a sense of failure.

Nana reached over and put a hand on her cheek. "Whatever comes, sweetie, what you've done is nothing less than a miracle."

Nana grabbed her robe and wrapped it around her. She kissed Finn on the head and headed out of the room. When Finn got back to the kitchen, Nana was already in the shed, getting herbs. Her mom was standing by Noah's bed, talking to him, hoping he'd talk back. Rafe stood there, like a sentinel.

Waiting was more than Finn could take. There had already been so much waiting. She grabbed her coat and phone and headed outside.

It was still dark. And cold, very cold. She breathed it in, felt her lungs react to the chill. The sun was just appearing on the horizon. She headed toward it, running for Jed's house.

His light was on when she got there. She texted: *I'm outside*. Through the window, she saw him stand up and look toward her. He disappeared, and a few moments later the front door opened. He ran outside. He was dressed but wasn't wearing shoes.

Jed picked her up and swung her around.

"You're okay!"

"Yes," she forced out, even though she could barely breathe. "Are you?"

"So very okay. Except for my feet, which are freezing." He set her down and looked in her eyes. "Did Noah wake up?"

"No. What if it doesn't work, Jed? What if, after all we went through, he doesn't wake up?"

"What if he does?"

He looked at her, nothing but joy on his face.

"What do you remember?" she asked.

"A bird. Lots of dark rooms."

"Caves."

"Caves. And it was cold," he added.

"Is that it?"

He nodded. "Am I missing something important?"

Her father.

But that was for later.

"Yes," she told him, smiling. "You were awesome."

He kissed her. "Of course I was. I'll get my shoes." He turned for his front door.

They ran back to her house. At moments, Jed was running so fast Finn was afraid he would yank her to the ground. But the one time she stumbled, he somehow sensed it and put an arm out to grab her.

They were both winded when they got to Finn's house. When they opened the door, a rush of warm air blew against them, keeping the chill outside.

Finn kept moving, heading straight for Noah's room.

Her mother stood on one side of his bed. Nana was next to her, rubbing an ointment on Noah's hands. It had a sweet smell, like a field full of clover. Rafe had taken a step back and now stood, helpless, behind Nana.

"Anything?" she asked, taking a spot on the other side of the bed.

"I thought he blinked," her mother said. "It might have been wishful thinking."

Finn reached out and grabbed Noah's free hand. Nana had already spread ointment on it. The skin was smooth. She leaned down next to her brother's ear.

Finn felt his breath against the side of her head.

In. Out. In. Out.

She loved him so much.

Noah had been gone so long, down in that cave, so small and scared.

"Noah," she said, "please come back. We're all here: Mom, Nana, Jed. Even Rafe is here. We love you, and we've missed you so much."

She waited. As she had all these months. Praying he would come back to her. Helpless to do anything . . . until she wasn't helpless anymore. She'd crossed another world to find him. It had to work.

"Finn?" It was whispered so quietly it was barely more than a breath.

She lifted her head so she could see Noah's face. His eyes were open. They were as blue as she remembered.

He looked at her . . . and smiled.

"Right here, Noah," she said. "I'm right here."

ACKNOWLEDGMENTS

Almost nothing in life is done by one person, and this book is no exception. Perhaps I deserve credit for having the original idea and for a whole lot of typing, but so much else about *River of Dreams* was either given or guided by others, a veritable flood of support and nurturing that I (we) could not have gotten through the last few years without.

So to Kathleen and Glenn Layendecker; Betsy and John Garibaldi; Yair Landau and Susan Purcell; Suzanne Bukinik; Jorge Estrada; Rosie Reyes; Maria Miranda; Sara(h) Meyer; Heather Meyer; Amy Resnick; Mike and Vicki Resnick; Milt Resnick; Ken Coleman; Kathryn Harrison; Greg Walker; Michelle Ashford; Maura Healey; the Milburn girls; Brad Falchuk; Ron McGee; Michael Sardo; Meg Hyman; Samantha Schlumberger; the Harari family; Stephanie Levine; Dorian Karchmar; Margaret Riley King; Blake Fronstin; Jamie Mandelbaum; everyone at Westwood Hills Congregational Church; Rick Commons, Jean Kaplan, and the entire Harvard-Westlake community; the writing staff of *Made in Jersey*; the writing staff of *Once Upon a Time in Wonderland*; Bill Haber, Angie Harmon, and the cast, crew, and writing staff of *Rizzoli & Isles*; Charles Holland, Mara Brock, Salem Akil, Adam Giaudrone, and the writing staff of *Black Lightning*; Chris Silber, Scott Bakula, and the cast, crew, and writing staff of *NCIS: New Orleans* ... thank you. For anyone I forgot to mention by name, I'm sorry. And thank you.

To Rina Mimoun and Jen Besser. This book would not exist without you. It would simply be a long, well-typed manuscript. So thank you for helping make it more.

To my dad, John, who loves me even if he doesn't understand me. I love you, too.

With a special shout-out to my sister, Julie, who is literally always there when I need her and provides gentle reminders not to stay "two years too long." Birds of prey know they are cool.

For Abe and Hazel, who asked me to write something they could read, here you go. You are both amazing, and I love you more than I have words to say, no matter how much I type.

And finally to Liz, my first reader, who gave notes I could actually hear on every single draft and kept saying she loved the book even when I was sick of it. You lived long enough to know I sold it, but not long enough to see it. I will never be able to look at the cover without thinking of you.